ORIGINAL WRITING

FROM

IRELAND'S OWN

2014

*Best of health
always*

RJ Poole

ORIGINAL WRITING

ISBNS
PARENT: 978-1-78237-652-1
EPUB: 978-1-78237-653-8
MOBI: 978-1-78237-654-5
PDF: 978-1-78237-655-2

A CIP catalogue for this book is available from the National Library.

Published by ORIGINAL WRITING LTD., Dublin, 2014
Printed by CLONDALKIN GROUP, Glasnevin, Dublin 11

INTRODUCTION

Ireland's Own, in conjunction with Original Writing, is delighted to bring to readers another anthology of the winners and other highly commended entries in our annual writing competitions. This is our fifth book and we are happy that this volume, drawn from the 2013 writing competitions run through the magazine, is again of a high standard, and we hope that you enjoy it.

Apart from our regular corps of professional and part-time contributors, Ireland's Own receives a great many unsolicited submissions every week, many of them of a very good standard. Writing has never been so popular and we do try to be sympathetic and encouraging in our approach, though we are only able to use a small portion of these submissions. We are constantly reminded of the great hunger there is out there among people to commit their ideas to print.

We have been running our Annual Short Stories and Memories Writing Competitions for many years, and they attract a very high-standard response. For the past seven years we have been supported in this by the self-publishing company, Original Writing, from Dublin, and their backing is greatly appreciated and our partnership with them has again made this anthology possible.

We congratulate the prize winners and all the other writers included; we thank them for their help and co-operation with this project and hope they are justifiably proud of the end result. We also compliment the hundreds of others who entered – perhaps you will have better luck in this year's competitions and will make it into the 2015 Anthology.

We meet a few old friends again in this collection, but there are a few others who are being published in a book for the first time and it is very special for them in particular. We wish all the writers future success if they pursue their writing ambitions. And Ireland's Own is happy to have played a part in helping you along the way.

A special word of thanks to international bestselling and much loved author, Alice Taylor, for providing us with a foreword for the book; her support and encouragement is greatly appreciated by us and our writers. She has had a long association with Ireland's Own and some of her early works were serialised in the magazine, including her iconic breakthrough book 'To School Through The Fields', still the bestselling Irish book of all time.

We thank former Ireland's Own editors, Gerry Breen and Margaret Galvin, for all their help with the annual competitions. We give a special word of thanks also to Martin Delany, Garrett Bonner, Steven Weekes and all the crew at Original Writing for their expertise and assistance.

The stories and memoirs in this book offer a good flavour of what can be enjoyed in the Ireland's Own magazine every week, along with many other regular features such as Song Words, Cookery, Jokes, Health and Lifestyle column, a substantial children's section and our old friends, Miss Flanagan, Cassidy and Dan Conway. We are very grateful to all those thousands of readers around the world who support the magazine every week, ensuring that we are still going strong after 112 years. Sure, The Week Wouldn't Be The Same Without It!

Phil Murphy and Sean Nolan
Ireland's Own

You can keep in touch with what's happening at Ireland's Own on our lively new website, *www.IrelandsOwn.ie*

ORIGINAL WRITING

Original Writing Limited ('OW') has had an association with Ireland's Own for a number of years both as sponsor of the magazine's writing competitions and as publisher of the 'Original Writing From Ireland's Own'. Over these years there have been many wonderful entries and it was with this in mind that we came up with the idea for the anthology. We would like to take this opportunity to congratulate all of the winners and other authors whose writings are contained in this anthology.

Original Writing Limited offers many different publishing, printing and eBook solutions which may be of particular interest to readers of Ireland's Own who also write in their spare time or have family members or friends who write.

OW can now give the writer an opportunity to have his or her work collected in one place and a paperback or hardback of bookshop quality with a full colour cover, produced by OW to distribute to family, friends and colleagues. Page counts can be as low as twelve and orders are accepted from five copies. Prices start at €2.65 per copy. For more information please go to www. originalwriting.ie

The market for eBooks is growing at a tremendous rate and we offer a conversion and listing service which will get the author's book listed on over 900 websites around the World.

We also offer websites for writers. Use our simple website builder to create a stylish, affordable and easily manageable online showcase for your work. Just go to www.originalwriting.ie for more information.

Contact Original Writing Limited at 01-6174834 or info@ originalwriting.ie. Further details are also available at www. originalwriting.ie

FOREWORD

BY ALICE TAYLOR

One of Ireland's most popular writers

Inspiration

"Imagination is evidence of the divine"

Hanging on the side of my kitchen cupboard is a plaque from The Wild Goose Studio in Kinsale with the above inscription. It is a quote from poet, philosopher and inspirational thinker, John Blake, who lived from 1757-182. I sometimes look at that quote and ponder on the depths of its wisdom. It causes me to deeply appreciate the gift of writing.

All creativity is a gift, be it writing, painting, music, gardening, baking, carving or whatever. This pool of creativity needs stimulation by use and it satisfies a deep inner need. If our pool of creativity is left to stagnate from lack of use it can die, but if kept flowing it will enrich our lives. Hence the joy in the gift of writing.

Every writer knows the delight of the right word fusing into the back of a barren mind, or the perfect sentence floating like a butterfly into a blank brain. Blake attributes this to the divine within us. What a glorious concept!

So before thought of publication comes into the mind of the writer, we already have had the delights of creativity. It is deeply satisfying to our inner being. When we have honed a piece of writing to our satisfaction, or finally got on canvas what was in the mind's eye, or see the first snow drop planted in the Autumn, thrust itself up through the bleak January earth, we experience the joy of creativity.

But for the writer then comes the need of recognition from our fellow humans. When I had my first manuscript accepted by a publisher, I danced with delight around the kitchen and sang "Alleluia". We writers have a deep desire to see our name in print. This Anthology provides that opportunity. Congratulations to all whose stories are glowing within.

Alice Taylor.

CONTENTS

HIGHLY COMMENDED

Between a Rock and a Hard Place
By Paul McLaughlin,
Belfast

Remembering a Belfast Summer illuminated by young love, punctuated by arguments about their differences and some lovely, precious times together

From a distance, Ballyholme Bay looked like a silver rock pool filled with toy boats, as little sails of blue, yellow and red bobbed up and down on the gentlest of swells. As far as the eye could see, the Sunday drivers of the nautical world, in their identical skipper hats and waterproof waistcoats, were hoisting, tacking and whistling for a wind as they ran on the spot.

A whisper of a Westerly crept round the point behind us as we ambled, arm over arm, toward the municipal tennis courts, our fish and chips obscuring the football features of Saturday night newspapers.

Your face was flushed with the sea air, with a child's eyes that sleep would ambush later and your hair hung still like silken shades framing your face. Shining black and fine like spun-thread on a dolly's head, it crashed to your slim shoulders like a dark wave, covering the scoop-neck of your embroidered blouse in a splash of black against the beaded scarlet of the velvet.

"You can be so ruddy immature", you screamed; "Jealous and childish and ruddy infuriating."

Your words cut me dead and I did not reply. My immaturity had grown silent and brooding, slipping sharp-faced into a sulk.

"Those boys are from college for heaven's sake, they're friends of mine" and your brows knitted as they surely would, permanently, in years to come.

I sensed that you were trivializing the matter and assumed that air of superiority that my mother found so annoying, while

1

trying to maintain my silence. But it was useless. My immaturity rushed from my throat in a stream of invective.

"The word is bloody. Not ruddy. Bloody. And some bloody friends they are. I've got loads of mates and they're all male. You know, proper school friends. You've got the front row of the first fifteen."

I could have cut out my tongue for showing my green hand of jealousy. It was clear for all to see that my argument was about to be tackled head high and kicked into touch. Your handling, as always, was impeccable.

"You just can't take it that some of my friends just happen to be boys. Aye and bigger boys than you. I didn't hear you say much to Trevor and William and the lads five minutes ago. You were all sweetness and light. Ruddy, I mean bloody, hale fellow well met. Sometimes, I think I must be the first girl you've ever known. You really want to catch yourself on."

Your straight right had caught me a crushing blow across the sensitive side of my ego. Yes, they were bigger than me, the whole shower of them, but they talked with marlies in their mouths and, anyway, we had fellas on our Gaelic team who would have beaten seven bells out of them before breakfast. More jolly hockey sticks than rugby, the whole lot of them. All 'daddy's car for the weekend' and big houses up the Malone Road. And all the other sort into the bargain.

I said nothing and tried to look unaffected. The darkness behind my eyes brooded heavily, weighing down my lids and threatening a torrent of tears.

"Seriously, Paul, you people live in a world of your own. Too many holy this and holy that and big bundles of guilt weighing you down. No wonder you can never join in."

I felt the familiar bile of an argument stirring in the back of my mouth. I made fists of sweating hands until the knuckles went white and lay down on the grass beside the crazy golf course. It seemed a more than appropriate place for my mood. Saying nothing was sometimes the best way. I remembered the wise advice from my father and how he reacted when my mother turned the air at home electric.

'Say nothing son and hide your head behind the evening paper. It works for me'. And, anyway, why should I allow myself to be dragged into a slanging match with somebody so obviously sectarian?

"Oh is that right?" I heard myself say. The pitch of the voice was just a little too high for a man of my machismo, the grip on my vocal chords about as weak as that on my temper.

"And I suppose some middle-class madam from the backend of Ballymacarrett knows more about how to behave than me... than I do. Is that it? Our people owned this country when your crowd was still chasing sheep outside Glasgow. And that includes your geeky friends with their bee-bap haircuts."

I felt I had done my tradition proud and managed a swipe at the Eton Wall gang into the bargain. "If youse don't like it here", and I stood tall like the young Pearse in that picture in the Ard Schoil, "There's nobody stoppin' youse going back where you came from."

My handle on Irish history was firm and unrepentant. There's one good thing about the Christian Brothers, they gave you ownership of your own history – no black or white, only green, especially when it came to arguing with Prods.

I didn't expect any comeback in the debating stakes and was surprised by her reaction.

"Forget all the stupid arguments about religion," she said gently; "Sure you know I'm High Church for heaven's sake and it is only a paper wall between us."

"Aye, a paper wall and a paper border too when it comes to it," as I fired a final volley for Ireland.

"Even your rugby hellions stand for 'The Soldier's Song'." I've seen them on TV looking tongue-tied and sheepish at Lansdowne Road." My last crow was that of the man who crows the longest.

Inside, I was annoyed that I couldn't remember the words of our anthem either in English or Irish – a bit like most people who attempt "Flower of Scotland" – but I felt ahead on points all the same. Brother Hanley had always said that a Protestant couldn't argue about Ireland, religion or anything but the "Twelfth" and he'd never been proved more right.

So, why did I not feel like a winner?

She sat down beside me, spreading the ankle-length mass of her denim skirt beneath her like a groundsheet, exposing a glimpse of white thigh as she turned to face me. "Give us a kiss and we'll call a truce," she said, babying me in a way that got my guard down and my blood up.

Brother 'H' had her number all right. An occasion of sin and no mistake. But then the good brother regarded all Protestant females as that and stated it constantly. It was always the best part of the Religious Instruction class when he dwelt on the sultry sins of the Orange femme fatale. I found myself wondering how he had gained such worldly experience when she suddenly used the killer word.

"Ach, dumdums, are we still friends?" It cut me through my sulk like silk and, curse it, a weak smile betrayed me. My weapons of spite and nationalism had been decommissioned and the war really was over. I had as good as said it. All the ejaculations to all the saints in the Jesuit calendar could not have saved me and I did not want them to.

"C'mere Orange Lil and give me a kiss". I took her lips as gratefully as many of our people had taken the soup and just as hurriedly. The taste of the sin was exquisite as we lay cuddled, our eyes closed tight and her breath fast and fiery above the collar of my Ben Sherman shirt. The argument had become flesh and was eagerly consumed. And the lime trees behind the grass courts swayed in the salt air like an enthralled audience.

Ballyholme, with its box hedges and pre-war villas, whose bowed windows caught and held the bay like rippling pictures, became our Sunday sanctuary from a city in flames. It was a middle ground in a world far away from the no-man's land that separated us at home.

Kipling was right when he described the differences between East and West. She had the Castlereagh Hills looking down benignly on her mother's neat little semi, while the scowl of the Black Mountain menaced my terraced home.

Her dad, in his RUC sergeant's uniform, remained on almost permanent border patrol between the two with a tongue like a trigger and a frown that he put on with his cap. But Ballyholme was a neutral zone that Summer, when August on our wall calendar at home burst into sectarian flames as fierce as the big map on the western TV show, Bonanza.

"We can be anything down there and no one will care," she said: "They even marry couples in both their churches – just to be sure, to be sure," and we'd laughed and leaned against each other for support. There had been no time to waste on further petty rows as summer slipped past in weekend instalments.

My wristwatch ticked away that Tuesday morning, close to my pulse as I waited for the post to arrive, closer to my heart as I read her letter 'end to start' as always. For ten weeks, this had been my way of reassuring myself of her feelings for me before enjoying the trivia of her words. And the perfume of the "*All my love, Lorraine*" in a flourish right at the end was a joy to inhale.

I breathed easily from the "*Dearest Paul*" opening, a little faster through the "*We're so different*" part and, with some considerable difficulty at the "*I'm too young to get into any kind of relationship*" bit. Tears fells heavy on the "*loveliest summer of my life*" line, but dark and terrible thoughts ate away at me as I read "*Perhaps in a few years we can meet again*".

I reached for my pen, determined to wound with words of revenge that would make mincemeat of her imperfections. No better man than me for a diatribe. She'd said so herself a hundred times. I'd send her off to her posh school, with all the other eejits from the collegiate, with a right face on her. But nothing came. No bile, no bitter phrases, no cut and dab, nothing.

Over a cup of cold tea and under the scrutiny of my perplexed mother, I pictured my Lorraine on the beach in July; the handful of freckles across her nose like grains of sand, the blue-black of her swimsuit making her skin look cool and creamy. The longing gripped my stomach in a cramp and I remembered her silly little romantic saying that "time fades everything except love".

In time, our faces would disappear from the Polaroid picture taken that Summer, but the memory of Ballyholme, of holding hands and hearts and hope, would remain remembered as a soft landscape of love between a rock and a hard place.

ALL THE COLOURS OF THE RAINBOW

BY LORNA COOPER,
Ballineen, Co. Cork

Olivia's shimmering silk dress was special to her and had been much admired by her father, with whom she had a special bond, and now she was wearing it to his funeral as a final tribute to him

Olivia stood by the living room window that overlooked the front lawn. She stared past the stately copper beech tree in a corner of the garden, oblivious to its magnificent foliage. In the room behind her, people were still coming and going, quietly shaking hands with the members of her family. They sympathized, and then retired to another room where tables were set up to provide refreshments for the mourners.

She fingered the neckline of her silk outfit with its shimmering rainbow colours. The elegant, cap-sleeved dress that just skimmed the knee had been perfect for a recent summer wedding. It had been the profusion of colours that had caught her eye the first time she had spotted it in the smart, new boutique in town. The material had no definitive pattern, just a subtle blending of colour that enhanced the overall visual effect. It had cost her a month's wages, saved from her holiday job in the local supermarket, but she considered it to have been worth every cent.

Earlier in the day as the family were preparing to depart for the church, her mother had frowned when she spotted Olivia's chosen outfit.

'Do you really think that you are dressed appropriately for such a solemn occasion?' she enquired with raised eyebrows.

'He liked this dress, especially the colours.' Olivia was almost defiant in her grief. 'He said I looked fantastic in it. I want to wear it for him today. I'm not changing now.' Her lower lip trembled in the face of her mother's opposition but she was determined not to give way. She owed her father that much, she thought.

As she heard her sigh, Olivia realised that her mother belonged to a generation that considered darker, more discreet clothing to be more suitable for a funeral, a family one in particular.

She thought again of the last time she had worn the dress; it had been for the wedding of a cousin, a splendid joyous occasion. She had just turned seventeen and had been delighted at the opportunity to wear a fashionable outfit of her choice, paid for with her own money. Still feeling defiant, she sensed that her mother, laden down with her own sorrow, was about to back down.

'Well, at least put on your navy jacket. That might tone it down a bit.' Julia was clearly weary and in no mood for further argument. Olivia had no option but to compromise. She left the room in silence and returned in a minute or two wearing her jacket over the dress. Peace was restored as she departed with her mother and younger brother to make the sad journey to the church.

The funeral service and the burial had passed in a blur for Olivia. She had struggled to sing the hymns and to get through her own reading but she had done it for her father. Later, in the graveyard when it was all over, she had stood beside her mother and Sean, shaking a multitude of hands as she accepted the standard "I'm sorry for your trouble." Trouble – the word was totally inadequate for how she felt today. It was not just trouble. It was sheer devastation.

Now Olivia could bear it no longer. She had an urgent desire to detach herself from the crowded room and to remove herself, however briefly, from its claustrophobic atmosphere. If she slipped away for a while, her absence would hardly be noticed. She took refuge in her bedroom and threw herself on the bed. Deep sobs engulfed her slim body as she lay face down on the duvet. She was not sure how long she had remained in that position. It was a gentle knock at the door that roused her.

'Olivia, are you in there?'

7

It was her Aunt Susan. For a moment she just wished that she could be left alone but she was fond of her aunt and did not want to appear ungracious.

'Yes, come in, Auntie.' She did her best to remain composed. Susan put her head around the door.

'Most people have gone home now. Just a few of the relations are still here. Are you okay? Maybe you should show your face for another while. I know it's hard but your mother expects it. Things are difficult enough for her too.'

There was a touch of concern in her aunt's voice.

'I understand that, but it's just…we seem to have been rowing a lot lately. She is always criticising everything I do, even the clothes I wear. She didn't want me to wear this dress to the funeral, you know. She seemed to think it was inappropriate. But Dad loved it. I wanted to wear it for him today. I still can't believe he's gone.' The tears welled up in Olivia's eyes once more.

Her aunt put her arm around her and tried to comfort her.

'Hush, now. Of course you're upset. I'm sure your Dad would have approved of you wearing your lovely dress. After all, as well as feeling sad that he's gone we were also celebrating his life. He'd have wanted you to look your best, really.'

'Thanks, Aunt Susan.' Olivia attempted a smile. How was it that her aunt always seemed to know the right thing to say to make her feel better? 'Tell Mum I'll be down in a minute.' Susan left the room, quietly closing the door behind her.

Olivia stood up and arranged the folds of her dress. She stood in front of the full-length mirror and noted once more how well it accentuated the curves of her body. The material softly skimmed her hips and shimmered as she turned sideways. The colours seemed to merge but the blues and yellows dominated.

'All the colours of the rainbow are in that dress,' her father had remarked as the family was about to depart for Marie and Ted's wedding. 'You remind me of a beautiful butterfly about to spread its wings and fly off in the sunshine. My little girl has grown into an elegant young woman.'

'My goodness, you'll be giving her a swelled head soon,' her mother had responded. 'What about the rest of us? Do Sean and

I meet with your approval?'

Olivia recalled her father's benevolent smile.

'Of course you do. You all look great. I'm very proud of my family. Now let's get going. We don't want to be late.'

At the reception, her father had danced with all the female members of his family. When he escorted Olivia to the floor, the band was belting out a lively rock and roll number. He was an excellent dancer and very light on his feet. He had already executed a graceful waltz with her mother and then had performed an up-tempo quickstep with one of his sisters.

Now he led Olivia into a fast jive that she loved. As he twirled her around, the dress swirled from side to side lifting upwards on the final swing to reveal her long, slim legs. At the end of the dance they had both collapsed onto their seats, flushed and laughing.

'That dress really suits you. You look just as pretty as the bride today. I'd be proud to walk you up the aisle some day.' His tone was light-hearted but she remembered his look of admiration.

Her laughter and response had been carefree. 'It's a bit early to be thinking along those lines, Dad. I don't intend to get married for years and years. I haven't even finished secondary school yet.'

'Yes, but that day will come eventually and when it does I'll be sorry to let you go but I'll definitely be the proudest man in town.'

For a moment she had wondered if the wine served with the meal had brought on this sudden sentimentality. Then she remembered that he was tee-total. The moment passed as he spotted her mother across the room, deep in conversation with Susan.

'Right, I'm off to take your mother for another twirl on the dance floor.'

He winked at her and was gone.

Olivia gazed sadly at her reflection. How she would miss him. She had always been a daddy's girl – perhaps too much so for her mother's liking. She fixed her shoulder length dark hair and went downstairs to bid goodbye to the remaining friends and relations.

Later they sat having a cup of tea; just the three of them. Olivia had changed into a comfortable pair of jeans and a white t-shirt. Sean had also dispensed with his funeral attire. He still looked shell-shocked, Olivia thought. He was only twelve, on the cusp of adolescence. Yet she did not know what to say that might comfort him. He finished his tea and then casually remarked:

'I'll just go on the computer for a while, Mum. Is that alright? I won't be long. Then I'll go straight to bed.' His mother hugged him.

'Of course, you do that. You were great today. Try to get a good night's sleep.'

As Sean left the room she sighed and turned to Olivia.

'The poor lamb. He's trying to act as normal as possible. It won't be easy – for any of us.' She looked sympathetically at her daughter. 'I'm sorry if I appeared short with you this morning. We were all under stress. You and I will have to try and pull together from now on, for Sean's sake if nothing else.'

Olivia nodded wearily. 'That's okay, Mum. I'll do my best. I think I'll go to bed too. I'm exhausted.' She said goodnight and retreated to the sanctuary of her room.

* * *

Her final exam results had arrived two weeks ago. Despite the difficult year since her father's death, Olivia had done well and would soon be leaving home to start a new life in college. Even her mother was pleased and had wholeheartedly congratulated her.

Now she was standing in front of her open wardrobe to begin sorting her clothes before packing. The rainbow coloured silk dress still hung at the end of the rail. She removed it from its hanger and carefully folded it. Then she placed it in a large bag and made her way to town.

The woman in the charity shop could not conceal her

admiration when she saw the dress.

'What lovely material. Pure silk, isn't it? The colours are brilliant. It looks new. I'd say this one will fly off the rail, no bother.'

Olivia nodded. 'It was only worn twice. I hope you get a good price for it.'

The woman thanked her and Olivia turned and left the shop. Yes, it had only been worn twice. The first occasion was one of joy; the other, one of sorrow. She could never wear that dress again. It had served its purpose.

She walked down the main street and stopped at the florist's shop. After much deliberation she chose a colourful mixed bouquet. There was one final trip she had to make before she was due to leave next day. She walked up the hill towards the parish church and its adjoining graveyard. She wandered along the pathway until she reached her father's grave. She cast her eye over the black marble headstone bearing the inscription to the memory of Michael Muldoon. She removed the previous, now almost withered blooms, from the vase and replaced them with the fresh flowers.

As she stood back to admire her arrangement, the sun suddenly broke through the clouds, dispersing the residue of a recent light shower. A magnificent rainbow appeared on the horizon. Olivia gazed in delight at the spectacle. Instinctively, she ran her fingers over the inscription of her father's name on the headstone.

'All the colours of the rainbow; I think they're shining just for you and me, Dad,' she whispered. Then, with one last backward glance, she left the churchyard to begin her new life.

11

SOAP OPERA
BY PADDY MURRAY,
Charlestown, Co. Mayo

Shaving with the cut-throat razor was a Saturday night ritual in many Irish homes in the old days.

With the invention of the electric razor, shaving has become an easy chore for the male of the species. A man can now shave almost anywhere, any time, on demand. Not the case in days gone by. In those days, shaving was a ritual that was done every Saturday night in preparation for Mass on Sunday morning.

My father's shaving kit consisted of three components: a cut-throat razor, a shaving stick and a shaving brush. A shard of a broken mirror perched precariously on a pointed end and propped up against a biscuit tin provided a mirror image of the theatre of operations.

Shaving was usually carried out by lamplight on the corner of the kitchen table. Given the poor lighting conditions and the type of razor that was used, it is nothing short of a miracle that a serious case of self mutilation did not occur.

Men of the land only shaved once a week - they did not believe in reaping until the stubble was at maximum strength and would not wilt before the blade. Only doctors, solicitors, insurance collectors and gardai shaved every day.

The shaving kit was usually kept in a biscuit tin on the dresser. Sometimes Herself would borrow the razor for emergencies and return it "gapped" to its case without a word. This would spark off an inquisition aimed at the entire household but mainly at Herself: "Who was using my bloody razor, was it you?" after the first stroke had drawn blood.

She, of course, would protest vehemently to the implied accusation and plead innocence of the first degree. The razor was then sharpened on the leather strop behind the kitchen door and the wound was repaired with a piece of The Enniscorthy Guardian newspaper.

The shaving session was usually heralded by the pronouncement "Don't use the water in that kettle; I need it for a shave!" Shaving was a soap opera and a surgical drama all in one. It required that the hands that milked cows, spread top dressing snagged turnips and guided the plough through the furrow, would temporarily morph into hands of surgical delicacy to facilitate the nature of the operation.

First the facial stubble was softened with hot water. A good foam was worked up and distributed thickly and evenly and then worked in with the shaving brush. The razor, having been previously stropped, was then applied with deft even strokes.

The open areas, sometimes referred to as "The headlands", were first cleared of stubble and the difficult area between the nose and the upper lip was left 'till last. This was a very sensitive area, and had to be navigated with surgical precision lest blood should be drawn.

The face was then rinsed with water, towelled off and inspected for miniscule cuts. This completed, the shaving kit was wiped dry and returned to the biscuit tin. The soapy water was thrown out the front door causing Herself to raise her eyes disapprovingly.

Thus was ended the shaving ritual for another week except when a midweek Macra meeting or a Hunt Ball arose and demanded a clean shaved visage to augment the collar and tie or the hired dress suit worn at such social gatherings.

The cut-throat razor was an example of precision, surgical ingenuity, and ergonomics, all engineered into one. Measuring seven inches in length, it was in two parts, the blade and the handle. Sheffield steel constituted the blade and the handle was mother of pearl.

The blade was little more than an inch wide and three inches long with a rounded back narrowing into a surgically sharp side which, sharpened to perfection could split a hair. The remainder of the blade extended into a curve like the letter "J". Into this curved portion fitted the little finger for stability while shaving. The handle also had a curved portion for the thumb to fit into and the whole unit folded up neatly for safety. The razor was kept in a molded case lined with blue velvet.

A razor man cared for his razor like a Samauri warrior cared for his sword. It was taken out from time to time for cleaning and it was sharpened with reverential care. The sharpening operation was done in two parts. First it was honed on an oilstone and then on the leather strop.

The oilstone was a rectangle of smooth grey limestone about eight inches long and three inches wide mounted in a rectangular block of wood. The razor was lightly rubbed on this stone for ten minutes and was lubricated from time to time with a light oil to give a smooth and surgically sharp finish. A final stropping concluded the operation. The razor was then polished, dried, and carefully replaced in its case.

Shaving nowadays is no longer the chore it used to be but rest assured, it will always be a necessity of life for the man of the house, because no sooner has the operation ended than the stubble will immediately begin to grow from the subcutaneous vaults beneath the surface of the skin.

The shaving procedure is never ending and will continue until the final crop of facial stubble has finally been harvested by the grim reaper himself.

THE CEILIDHERS
BY ROSE JOY PARKE,
Enniskillen, Co. Fermanagh

A lovely evocation of country days gone by when people called on each other and made their own entertainment, with music, dancing and fun

I could hear the till jangling and the farmers laughing in the shop below my bedroom, so it must have been past nine o'clock. I could smell the sweetness of the walnut plug tobacco that Packy Flanagan was smoking, as it seeped up through the floorboards but maybe I was only imagining it.

I jumped out of bed, pulled on a pair of faded red shorts and an old white T-shirt and called to my brother Charles to get up. Downstairs, Bridie, the maid, was frying bacon and eggs and fadge bread on an old cream Aga that my grandparents had been given as a wedding present.

We ate quickly, then pulled on socks, wellingtons and windcheaters and sat outside on the window sill to wait impatiently for Paddy to come from the creamery. I drew squares on the footpath and we played hopscotch for half an hour but we were too excited at the prospect of our ceilidh to concentrate any longer.

We watched donkeys and carts rumble to and fro up the street to the creamery at the top of the village. Finally, we saw Paddy coming down the street with his cap sitting rakishly on the back of his curly chestnut hair, wearing his older black suit and a pair of turned down black wellingtons.

We kissed mammy goodbye and climbed into the cart, two fair haired, blue eyed, rosy cheeked children. We sat on the floor of the cart, on either side of Paddy. "Gee up" said he, and off we trotted. It was Saturday morning and we were off to stay with Meeky and it was the best morning of the week.

The old jinnet trotted slowly for the mile and three quarters journey. We turned up the road to Meehan's house, up a steep brae with hedges full primroses, violets, and woodbine, and there was Meekys, down in the hollow.

The entrance to the farm was between two beautiful pillars adorned with broken fragments of old blue glass, Belleek delph interspersed with shells that Bridie had picked off the beach in Bundoran. Sure, the pillars were a work of art.

There was Meeky standing, waving at us from the back door; she was a tall heavy boned woman with white hair pulled back into a bun, a smiling rosy face with ill fitting false teeth. Like all country women she was wearing a wraparound black apron, with sprigs of flowers in cornflower blue, under which she wore a black blouse and long black woollen skirt and stockings. On her feet, a pair of sturdy black boots laced up to the ankles.

We climbed off the cart and ran to hug her. She told us to wash our hands because we were soon to have our dinner. The tin basin was filled with cold water and the red lifebuoy soap was in a cracked saucer on the old wooden bench by the back door. Behind the back door was the roll towel, as grey as the tin basin, and as usual, I sniffed its dampness and breathed in its peculiar sour milky smell and I was completely content.

Opposite the back door was the front door, alongside which stood a well worn velvet chaise longue, under the window, and above which hung a wooden cage, in which a linnet was singing. The range was black leaded and had a brass tap on its boiler and beside that was an ancient armchair covered with a patchwork bedspread.

Beside the back door was the deal table, under a window, which was covered with a lacy curtain and around which we all now sat, awaiting our favourite dinner; mashed priddies with a pool of Knockmore butter in a well in the middle, and a fried egg and a tin porringer of cold milk, fresh from the lean-to whitewashed dairy, and no vegetables. Man a dear – what a treat. Pudding was always rice and tinned peaches.

Then Meeky brought in the tin basin and washed delph with boiling water from the range, and I brushed the flagstone with a turkey wing, sweeping the dust under the range, just the way

Paddy did. That done, Charles helped Paddy brush out the byre, and I gathered the still warm pullet eggs from the Parkes tea chest in the hen house and pulled my t-shirt to form a pouch in which to contain them.

I took them to the kitchen and Meeky cleaned them with baking soda on a damp rag, before depositing them into a wicker basket, ready to be taken to our shop on Monday morning, to exchange for flour, sugar, tea and butter.

We had only just finished when I heard Bridie approaching, singing "Mocking Bird Hill" as she hurried down the lane to the back door. Bridie was a maid no longer but Queen in her own kitchen. She took a bag of flour from her basket and set it on the oilcloth before she took off her green tweed coat, one which had belonged to my mother, and the scent of mammy's perfume still lingered around its collar.

I washed and dried the tin basin for Bridie and put in two porrngers of buttermilk from the cream and blue striped stripped delph jug. I stirred the bread mixture with a wooden spoon and Bridie piled it into a battered baking tin and put it into the oven. It was to be kept for the ceilidh, later in the evening, which was going to be mighty craic altogether.

The Angelus rang at 6 o'clock in Derrygonnelly and we could hear it clearly. Meeky and Bridie blessed themselves and said a wee prayer. At long last the clock struck nine. Charles and I were sent out to the shough to pee and as I straddled the shough, I could smell the turf smoke from the chimney and the sweet lingering fragrance of the woodbine that wound its way up the gable wall.

Then we had to wash our hands in the tin basin and combed our hair with Paddy's comb that was always coated in Vaseline hair tonic. Then we put on our pyjamas and waited in anticipation for the ceilidh.

As always I watched Paddy getting ready to go courting. He pulled down his braces and took off his old shirt, lathered his hands with lifebuoy soap, and slapped it around his face, ears and neck. Oh the smell of it. That done he put on a clean blue and white striped shirt that Meeky had warmed over the range.

17

Then he cupped his hands to put a wet pool of Vaseline tonic into his palm, and spread it over his chestnut curls, before combing them back behind his ears. Man a dear, he was so handsome, just like one of those film stars you could see on the screen in the Regal cinema.

At nine o'clock the back door knocked and the ceilidhers arrived - Steven M'Ateggart with his accordion and Seamus Dolan with his fiddle wrapped in a piece of black cloth tied with a bit of twine. In their black suits, black boots and Donegal tweed caps pulled down over their foreheads, they were very smart altogether.

Both Tilly lamps were lit, one in each window, and the two pulled up two wooden kitchen chairs in front of the range, hooked their green caps over their knees and proceeded to play reel after reel. The session had begun. Bridie danced, Meeky danced, we danced, the lamplight danced, the shadows danced, and the linnet went to sleep.

The session ended at 11 o'clock and we had the squib, porringers of strong, sweet Parkes tea and the fresh fadge with rhubarb jam were passed around. Bridie wound up the Gramophone and put on a masters voice record 'On top of old Smokey' with us all singing along. Bridie Gallagher sang 'Beautiful Bundoran', and my Bridie sang along with it; the lamplight suffusing her lovely jolly face in a pool of gentle rosiness.

The antique American clock on the wall above the range chimed midnight and Charles and I were sent upstairs to Bridie's big bed, to sleep on a feather tick, sheets made from flour bags, and under an eiderdown full of duck feathers, sewn up by Meeky, me at the top and Charles at the bottom for Bridie was a big woman and needed plenty of room.

As we nestled in bed by candlelight, we listened to the folk in the kitchen below as they recited the mellifluous rosary in whisperings that floated up the staircase and lulled us in to the sleep of innocents and innocence.

Under The Stairs
By Mary Cassoni,
Dun Laoghaire, Co. Dublin

*The space under the stairs was where anything and everything could
be found in many houses, a treasure chest or a dumping ground,
depending on your point of view*

In our house when I was a child if an item was missing it was
under the stairs. If it was hidden it was under the stairs. If it
was of any value or likely to be used again, it was under the
stairs. This large space had a small door into it from our living
room. You had to go on your hands and knees to enter. All kinds
of everything were kept there.

Among the treasures were two flat irons used to iron our
clothes. The iron was heated on the gas stove and while one was
being used the second iron was heating in readiness. My mother
tested the iron for heat by spitting on the base; if it sizzled it was
hot enough.

Stored there also was my father's shoe last. This was made
from cast-iron and every so often my father would buy leather
and with a shoe on the last would remove the worn sole and
heel with a pliers, cut the new leather approximately to size and
tack it on to the shoe or boot with a small hammer and nails
that he held in his mouth.

He would then trim the leather into shape with a sharp knife.
Many an expletive was learned by us children when the knife
slipped as it often did.

My mother's washboard, a wooden board made from ash
with grooves in it, was removed every Monday morning from
under the stairs and placed in the old square sink, and with a
bar of carbolic soap my mother scrubbed our clothes by rubbing
them up and down the washboard. She was always very proud
of her 'whites' blowing in the wind on the clothesline.

Some years later an enterprising neighbour rented out 'twin

tubs' for half a crown an hour. This was real luxury for my mother when she could afford it. The washing would always be done in a hurry as only one hour could be afforded.

The family hot water bottle was kept under the stairs and as I was the youngest child I was sent to bed first. I got the stone bottle filled with boiling water with a towel wrapped around it for safety and put in my bed. After a while my mother would change it into my brother's bed and finally it was put in my parents' bed.

By this time the towel was discarded as the bottle had cooled down considerably. But no way was the kettle boiled again to refill it.

All our old soap ends were kept in a jar which when full would be melted down over boiling water and made into new soap bars. Occasionally a new bar of soap would be added to the bits left to renew the supply.

Old newspapers were saved and they became our supply of toilet paper. They were cut into squares, and hung on cord from the cistern, one was always told to "spare the paper".

Money was not plentiful in our house and my parents though never mean were very thrifty. Our heating comprised of an open fire with logs cut up by my father. There were always a few logs kept for emergencies under the stairs. He was also known to cycle to the bog up the Dublin Mountains and bring home the turf he cut in a bag on the handlebars of his bicycle.

A very important day in our home was the day the money from the gas meter was collected by the gas man. The gas meter was fitted into a corner under the stairs. My mother saved her shillings and put one into the meter as required. When the gas man came he emptied the meter box onto the kitchen table to count the shillings. Getting into the meter was often a struggle for him depending on his waist-line.

My mother and my brothers stood by watching him count while I had to stand up on a chair to get a good view. The gas man built the coins into heaps of one pound and depending on the amount counted my mother was given back a refund of four or maybe five shillings. These were carefully put away in the jar for further use. Then the gas man was given a cup of tea and he went on his way.

In 1987 shortly after my father died, on tidying out this 'Aladdin's Cave' under the stairs we found a jam jar with over three hundred pounds cash and an insurance policy which was to cover his burial. You see, my late father never trusted the banks... In hindsight he was indeed a very wise man.

THE HOUSE
BY BRIAN MCCABE,
Johnstown, Co. Kildare

*All seemed right with the world for a young couple when they
spotted the ruined old house on a site that seemed to have lots of
potential; it was just the place to build their dream home ...*

It was just a ruin, really, when we first saw it. The roof had
obviously fallen in many years before and the walls had
started to unravel. It was in a nice position, though, with
mature trees all around and a little lake on the other side of the
road. An old hayshed rusted to one side.

We always passed it on our way to visit Debbie's parents up
country and we often commented on how nice it would be to
build a new house on the site, one that we could design ourselves.
We could see ourselves raising children there, that was one thing
we were agreed on.

At the time, Debbie was working for the building society. It
was expanding and issuing more loans each year. Profits were
growing and, as a staff member, Debbie would be able to get a
loan at a special rate. That would not be a problem. My business
was booming as well. I now had two men working for me and
was thinking of taking on a third to handle the extra work
which I was now having to turn down.

Gradually, our idle dreaming began to become more than
that. We found out who owned the land and after much
negotiation, bought the old ruin and two acres of land around
it, which included the trees. The farmer drove a hard bargain
but Debbie had her heart set on building there and, anyway,
wasn't property the best investment there was? We were both
agreed - it was our investment in our joint future.

I had known that it would be difficult to get planning
permission to build what they termed "one-off" housing in that
area, but a friend of my father's had said that the way to get

around that was to buy an old existing house and apply for permission to do it up. That made it very difficult for the County Council to refuse permission.

He was right. After an inspection and about six months of tortuous "discussions" with planning officials, we got permission to restore the old house and, most important of all, to extend it "in a sympathetic manner". Mind you, we had to hire a planning consultant to deal with the Council's planning department and there were legal costs and levies which I had not anticipated, but I knew it would be worth it in the long run.

We had walked, proudly, around the site on the day after the sale had been finalised. Debbie knew exactly where she wanted everything to go in the new house.

"We can have the living room here and the kitchen over there; a good big one, and I want it to catch the sun in the morning. I know exactly how I want it fitted out. I know we said three bedrooms but I think we should add another, in case any of our friends want to stay overnight. It's a good bit from the city here."

I smiled indulgently. "We'll see what we can do".

I knew the planning permission only allowed for extension at the back and that it could not be any higher than the height of the old house, but I was sure we could work something out once we got going. After all, as old Tom had said: "Once ye have it built, they can hardly make ye knock it again" and, he added with a wink "Sure, as the wise man once said, isn't it easier some times to ask for forgiveness than for permission?"

He was right. The Council never came near us. I had another look at the plans. If we simply demolished the old house, we could have a much wider road frontage and include all the features we wanted. I made sure to hold on to all the old stones, even though the builders wanted to take them away. We could use them for the new garage beside the house, where the old hayshed stood. It would save a few bob – especially as the cost of our dream was now beginning to mount up.

I had plenty of friends in construction, so I knew that the building itself would not be a problem, but I had underestimated how busy they all were. I ended up having to do a lot of the initial work myself, but at least I could use their VAT numbers for materials – which was just as well, because every time I went back to the wholesalers for something, it seemed to have gone up in price.

The year dragged on and I could see that Debbie was growing impatient. Each weekend when we travelled that road, we stopped and paced around the site, reviewing progress and renewing our dream. The first time, she looked a bit dubiously at the old stones, piled in a heap to one side of the site.

"It seems a shame to have knocked it all down" she said. "Could we not have used them somehow?"

She cheered up when I told her about the new two-car garage I was planning alongside. "They'll make a nice feature" I reassured her.

That winter was hard, frosty and then heavier snow than either of us could remember. The skeleton of our new house stuck up through the drifts of snow and we worried about the damage it might be doing to our untested foundations and unfinished block work. Only the old stones seemed impervious – a stubborn white cairn crouched under the snowy winter blanket.

Spring came and went and the countryside sprang to life again, but it was a different life. Our old world had collapsed. Debbie's employers featured in the daily news bulletins. Their days were numbered. She was one of the last to be let go, but let go she was. My business was also beginning to dry up. Soon I had to let both of my friends go.

I apologised to them the morning I told them but they said they understood. They had seen it coming. I heard later that both of them left for Australia shortly afterwards.

The only good thing about the situation was that I now had time to devote myself to finishing the house. I congratulated myself on buying as much of the materials as I had, even at the exorbitant prices. There was no way now that I would be able to get that bank loan which I had been planning to apply for.

I began to work at the house almost every day, and sometimes late into the night. It kept me busy and gave me something to focus on. It also kept me from listening to the ever-louder daily drum beat of despair emanating from the television and radio. I had given up buying newspapers long since. Nothing there but bad news. In fact, we had both found ourselves giving up lots of things that we would have regarded as essential the year before.

We gave up one of the cars and then, a few months later left the apartment in the city, with its great view of the Grand Canal Dock. We said farewell to the silver Spire, with its evening-time glint on the horizon. Debbie moved back to live with her parents and began to look for work, even a part time job, locally. Nothing doing.

I came home one evening to find her looking worried and puzzling over the title deeds of the old house. "Don't worry" I said "The solicitor checked it out. Everything is in order. The sale has been registered. I've checked it myself"

"No, it's not that" she said "It's just that I was talking to a woman in the shop today and when I told her about our site, she said that it was unlucky"

"Unlucky, what did she mean?"

"I don't know. I asked her what she meant but she just shook her head and left. The shopkeeper said he didn't know anything about it"

I worked through the summer and took to sleeping in the shell of the new house when, eventually, myself and a friend (who now had time to help me) managed to put a roof of sorts on it. I had underestimated how many slates we would need when placing the original order.

The extra bedroom, and the planned children's playroom which Debbie and I had later added to our mental map, were now out of the question. We managed however, to salvage some of the slates of the old house, from where they had been dumped in the field, and finished it – after a fashion. At least it would keep the rain out. I could come back to it later.

I thought I would enjoy sleeping there but, somehow, my sleep always seemed to be fitful. By now, our mortgage was well in arrears and the bills were beginning to mount up. I juggled them for as long as I could. The wholesalers were being completely unreasonable and insisting on full payment on all accounts immediately. I offered to agree a schedule of payment. They threatened to take back the materials. One of them said he would report me to "The Revenue". I told him he was welcome to do that.

Debbie was becoming obsessed with the history of the old house and what the old woman had said to her. She had begun talking to everyone in the area and asking them if they knew why our site was regarded as unlucky. Mostly, they just shook their heads but one old couple told her, gently, that it was "better to let the past lie".

I was spending more and more time in the house. I was borrowing from my family now for anything I bought. The heap of old stones seemed to mock me every time I drove out onto the road, on another begging mission. As the weeks went by, I found myself eating less and less. My clothes were going unwashed for longer periods. Everything I had was going into the house. I was determined to have something to show for my troubles at the end of the day.

I was now beginning to get post at the new address, but mostly they were just bills, or final notices. As my birthday approached, I got one or two cards, a pleasant change from the constant diet of demands which I had grown used to. I recognised my mother's handwriting on one of the envelopes and, sure enough, when I opened it, there was a cheque inside. Silently, I blessed her. That would pay for a few bags of plaster for the front room. Maybe Debbie could move in soon.

Next morning I woke early, determined to make a positive start to what looked like being a bright sunny day. The postman arrived, this time with an official looking envelope. For a moment, I thought about not opening it until I came back from town with the plaster.

It was from the bank who had taken over Debbie's building society the previous year. Having ignored me for the previous twelve months, despite my many phone calls, they were now advising me that, in their view, I would not be in a position to repay the loan and that the new house would have to be sold.

I was still sitting at the table when Debbie called in about two hours later.

I looked up tiredly. Her face was ashen. "I've discovered why our house is unlucky" she whispered

She laid down a photocopied A3 page in front of me. She had been in to the local library that morning and asked if they had anything on the history of our area. They had found a report in the local paper dating from the 1880s.

A photograph of the old house stared back at me from the top of the page. It was still pretty much intact then, but it had an ugly gash in the side of the front wall, clearly caused by the battering ram which was pictured suspended from a wooden tripod standing before the front door. A group of policemen in pointed helmets stood staring balefully at the camera lens, frozen forever in the middle of their destructive task.

A well dressed man, in a wing collar and wearing a top hat, stood to one side, clearly directing operations.

My eyes travelled slowly to the page underneath. The headlines told the story.

"Sad Scenes at Local Eviction!!!"

"Bailiff and Constabulary quell disturbances!!"

"Family ejected from Homestead!"

And I knew then, with absolute certainty that Debbie would never move into our new house.

The Girl With The Flaxen Hair
By Joe Spearin,
Clonlara, Co. Clare

He looked forward to seeing 'his girl' pass along the street every day, a constant pleasure in the ever-changing seasons of the year. Quite suddenly she no longer appeared and he missed her fleeting presence ...

He saw her each morning, coming towards him on the busy city street. They would pass each other at the bakery or near the cafe or outside the flower shop. She was a tall girl, attractive, and she had flaxen hair that shone in the early light. He guessed her age to be in the mid to late twenties, much younger than himself.

Sometimes, with the sun behind her, the outline of her form would be silhouetted against the shimmering haze of dawn. On such occasions he would think of Shakespeare's words: 'But soft! What light through yonder window breaks? It is the east and Juliet is the sun.' He didn't know if her name was Juliet. In fact he knew very little about her at all but it didn't bother him. The only thing that mattered was her presence on the street.

He first saw her in April, when the trays containing the new green shoots were being placed outside the flower shop in order to catch the sunlight. Now it was June and all the shrubs and seedlings had blossomed into a striking display of colour. A rainbow assortment of flowers spilled over the rims of hanging baskets, roses, lilies and chrysanthemums vying for space in their overcrowded containers.

He had a fondness for this street. It had character, he thought. He could have walked the entire length of it with his eyes closed and still have known where he was, using his nose as a guide. The bakery, cafe and flower shop all had their own distinctive smells. He loved passing by the fishmongers where the salty tang of sea-fresh produce tickled his nostrils. A sign, sellotaped to the window, told would-be customers 'if it swims, we sell it.'

The facades of all the premises were kept in good order, the owners taking pride in the appearance of their properties. The crèche, at the end of the street, had its frontage decorated with images of cartoon characters and smiley faces.

Most of the early-morning commuters tended to focus on getting to their place of work, moving along the street in a determined manner, oblivious to any distraction. Some people took chances at times, crossing to the other side through gaps in the traffic.

The girl with the flaxen hair noticed things. He saw her look upwards on one occasion to where some sparrows were squabbling in the eaves overhead the butcher's shop. He saw her smile as well at the hesitance of a nervous cat, poised at an alley-way threshold.

Such sensitivity to the ordinary was a rare quality, he reckoned. The simple things in life were often the most precious.

He thought he saw the lilies blush one morning as she passed by the flower shop, something that didn't really surprise him. She was far more beautiful than any cultivated bloom, but then he would have to admit he was biased.

He imagined that young students, who encountered her on their way to college, would be inspired to compose essays extolling her loveliness. Handel could have had someone like her in mind when he wrote 'Where 'ere you walk, cool gales shall fan the glade, trees where you sit shall crowd into a shade.'

He avoided eye contact with her, preferring not to risk any familiarity. By and large, there was a protocol of non-involvement amongst people who passed each other on busy city streets. It was an etiquette that was comforting to him. Anonymity allowed him the privilege of observing without complication. Those who saluted acquaintances did so with a cheery 'good morning,' or 'hello there'.

He realised that any acknowledgement of the girl's presence by him, whether by a polite smile or a nod of his head, would diminish the thrill and excitement of his secret worship.

He had a dream one night in which he saw the girl coming

towards him on the street, her flaxen hair glowing in the sunlight. He saw a red rose on the ground. It had fallen from one of the hanging baskets outside the flower shop. He picked it up and handed it to her and she smiled.

In the dream, he sensed that she was about to thank him but he put a finger to his lips and shook his head. She walked away, still smiling and glancing occasionally at the rose held lightly in her hand. The image faded and he woke up refreshed.

As summer progressed she grew more alluring, her countenance radiant and glowing, her demeanour and carriage indicative of good health and well-being. She had become an important part of his morning. He found the experience of seeing her each day to be inspiring and stimulating. It set the tenor for the even passage of his daily chores.

Her summer attire was appropriate for the season. She was never overdressed, nor did he ever notice any profusion of make-up on her features. Her deportment was that of someone who was used to regular walking and he often thought she would look well strutting along a catwalk, modelling clothes.

Autumn had that restful ambience that comes when there is a slowing of tempo in nature's course. The street assumed a mellow tone that was pleasant and relaxing. The sycamore and chestnut trees lining the pavement showed tinges of yellow, red and brown in their foliage.

Towards the end of September, with the mornings getting cooler, the girl wore a three-quarter length coat, a new addition to her ensemble. Her gait seemed more relaxed on these mornings and he assumed that she was absorbing the autumnal splendour that was all around her.

In October he took a week's holiday. The weather was bad. It rained every day and he spent most of his time indoors, reading books and watching television. At the end of the week there was a storm that lasted all day on Sunday. He was looking forward to going back to work.

Monday morning was calm. A watery sun shone down on the street where the after-effects of the storm were all around. Council workers swept fallen leaves and debris into neat piles ready for collection by refuse trucks.

Outside the bakery, a man on a ladder was busy securing part of a metal chute that had been dislodged by the gales. The fishmonger's window was being cleaned by one of the young counter assistants. All the business premises were open and trading. Something was missing, however. There was no sign of the girl.

She didn't appear on the following day or any other day of that week, or the week after. As time went by he became resigned to the notion that she had moved on to another job, maybe at some other location. The joy of seeing her each day was a thing of the past.

During her brief sojourn as a commuter on the street she had made a lasting impression on him and though she may have been unaware of his admiration, he knew that a candle would always burn for her in the cathedral of his heart.

The first snow of winter came in December and the street assumed a seasonal look, just like those scenes depicted on Christmas cards. He loved Christmas. With so much good feeling abroad it was a pleasure to be out and about, absorbing the Christmas atmosphere.

During the holiday period he visited churches to view the cribs, something that he had always done since his childhood when his parents were alive. Some churches had made special efforts to have the nativity scene seem as lifelike as possible. In one church, where the crib was located beneath the organ loft, the viewing area was cramped and he stood back, waiting for people to move away after they had finished paying homage to the depiction of the saviour's birthplace.

A woman, kneeling at the crib, stood up and made the sign of the cross. As she turned to leave, he noticed that she was wearing a mantilla and through the thin lace he saw her flaxen hair, cut in the same style as his 'lost' girl and he was reminded of her.

The dark mornings and gloomy days of January went by slowly. The street had a bare look. Doors were kept closed against the cold weather. People hurried to the warmth and shelter of their work places.

The lengthening daylight of early spring seemed to lift the spirits of commuters. The first daffodils of the season arrived at the florist's shop.

On a Monday morning in March he was later than usual making his way along the street. He had dallied over his breakfast and as he breezed past the butchers and the cafe his focus was on getting to work on time, or as near to it as possible. He dashed past the flower shop and the fishmongers.

As he came to the crèche the door opened and a young woman began to back out. She was waving to someone inside the premises. He saw her too late and they bumped into each other, shoulder to shoulder. She turned around and he saw her face, the face of 'his girl', as lovely as ever and blushing in her embarrassment. "I'm so sorry" she said, "it was my fault entirely. It's my new baby's first day in the crèche and I was saying goodbye to her."

He smiled, dismissing her apology with a wave of his hand and he stepped aside, allowing her to pass by. "Sorry again" she said and then she was gone.

He waited until she was past the fishmongers before he walked away. He was still running late and he hoped that his lack of punctuality would go unnoticed at the school for the deaf where he worked as a teacher, the same school he attended as a child.

Memories Runner-Up

THE STRANGER
BY LINDA GUERIN
Aspen Gardens, Limerick

*A caller to a Limerick house in the 1960s left a lasting impression
on a childhood memory*

It was autumn in the early 1960s; the weather had been stormy for several days, but that morning the wind had moderated and a fine, soft rain fell on Limerick city. I was about four or five years old as I sat in the kitchen of my family's terraced house.

A few sticks and a shovel of coal crackled in the small fireplace. The valve radio in the corner played Irish ballads and songs from Hollywood musicals. My mother read a newspaper and I was engrossed in a girl's comic. Then someone knocked at the door.

I followed my mother into the hall and watched her open the front door. A tall, thin man stood on the footpath. An air of mystery hung about him as if he had travelled a long distance, yet he carried no bag.

The stranger's long, black hair hung down from a grey, brimmed, felt hat and dripped rainwater on his upturned collar. His voluminous, double-breasted overcoat stretched almost to his ankles and afforded him good protection from the elements.

At first glance the man reminded me of one of the eighteenth century buccaneers that I had read about in my comics. He could easily have fitted into the crew of Blackbeard or Calico Jack Rackham who had sailed the seven seas, raiding merchants' ships and amassing hoards of treasure. All the stranger lacked was a cutlass at his side to complete the image of an adventurer.

"Have you anything that needs mending, ma'am?" he asked quietly. He spoke almost in a whisper. "Has a knob come off a lid? Or a pan lost its handle?"

My family lived in a row of four houses. The row was

approximately twelve feet wide and it was so insignificant that it rarely appeared on maps of the city. Yet, every day large numbers of pedestrians tramped up and down the narrow street. Some people were taking a short cut to William Street; others were factory workers hurrying home after work. There were several food processing factories in the centre of Limerick in those days.

My mother calmly met the stranger's dark eyes. "Wait a moment," she said. Leaving me to hold the front door, she withdrew to the kitchen. I wondered what broken, household item she had in mind to give the stranger.

A short time later my mother appeared with a navy and red umbrella that had blown out in a recent gale. The stranger nodded his head, took the umbrella and walked in a slow, dignified manner to the end of the row. There the man sat down on the wet footpath, using the tail ends of his overcoat as a makeshift ground sheet.

Before the front door closed I saw the stranger produce tools from the deep pockets of his overcoat and patiently set to work. He seemed oblivious to the soft rain that was falling or to the curious glances of passers-by.

In the kitchen my mother stoked up the fire with another shovel of coal and put on the kettle to do the washing up. I took out my little schoolbag and started to do the sums that my teacher had set as homework.

About ten minutes later there was another knock. My mother opened the front door again. I stood at her side. The stranger had returned with the umbrella. He demonstrated that it was in working order before he handed the item to me. My mother thanked him and put a few coins into his hand.

The stranger nodded his head and walked quietly away to the end of the row, turned the corner and disappeared out of sight.

THE BIRTHDAY WISH
BY PAULINE DODWELL
Edmonton, London

Pascal was used to being the top of the class in most things, but then a new rival came on the scene to threaten his number one rating ...

Birthday wishes didn't always come true. That was an undeniable fact and Pascal Davitt knew it from personal experience. Over the past six years, only the wishes he'd made on his fifth and seventh birthdays had come true. Now, contemplating the exquisite cake in front of him, Pascal was particularly anxious for a change in his luck.

"Hurry up and make a wish", his sister Alice urged, eyeing the cake.

Pascal thought for a moment. He made *two* wishes: the first that he would win the hundred yards sprint on Sports Day; the second, that Rosaleena Flanagan would not!

It was the twenty-fifth of June, 1958 and it was Pascal's tenth birthday.

Rosaleena Flanagan lived in the Big House at Rathallan. She was the only child of Neely and Sarah Flanagan who had moved up from Dublin in January when Neely inherited the property from his Great Aunt Louisa.

Rosaleena soon made her mark in the school. Pascal had seen her in the juniors' playground organizing her classmates in this or that game, coercing and cajoling them by turns. She was bossy and demanding and Pascal was thankful he was in the senior class and well away from her overbearing presence.

His complacency was short-lived. The first day back at school after Easter, Headmaster Foley walked into the classroom with Rosaleena in tow. A ripple of excitement spread along the rows of desks, pupils nudging one another, whispering and mumbling.

"Quiet!" Master Foley's voice rose above the din. The cacophony died away.

"Face the front", Master Foley commanded. All heads turned towards him. "Now, boys and girls", he continued, "You all know Rosaleena here. Well, she is going in for the Scholarship and she's joining this class from today". The whispering began again.

Master Foley raised an admonishing hand. Rosaleena stood beside him, head up, haughty, her gaze unwavering.

"Peter Nolan", Master Foley addressed the boy next to Pascal in one of the double desks along the wall. "You go over and sit beside Sally Dunne". Peter stood up. Pascal moved out on to the aisle and let him pass.

"Now, Rosaleena, you go and sit beside Pascal Davitt there", Master Foley instructed.

Rosaleena curled her lip. "Do I have to sit beside a young filla?" she asked scornfully. "Young fillas are such a heart-scald".

"Do you want to go in for the Scholarship?" Master Foley retorted.

"I do, surely!" declared Rosaleena.

"Well, then", Master Foley told her curtly, "You'll sit where you're put".

Rosaleena threw up her head but in prudent compliance strode down the schoolroom to the allocated desk. Pascal stood aside to let her sit by the wall.

"No", Rosaleena said brusquely, "I'll sit by the aisle".

"But this is *my* seat", Pascal protested, "I always sit on the outside".

"Well then it's *my* turn now", Rosaleena whispered fiercely. "Move over".

All heads turned in their direction, a frisson of excitement ruffled the air.

"Quiet!" Master Foley, writing on the blackboard, did not turn round. "I don't want to hear another word".

Pascal stood his ground. Rosaleena fixed him with an unblinking gaze.

"Right!" she hissed. "If you don't shove over, I'll sit on your knee".

Pascal hesitated a moment. Then he sat down and slid over

to the wall. Rosaleena took her seat with a self-satisfied smile. Presently, she opened her satchel and took out a pencil-case and jotter. Placing them on the desk in front of her, she turned to Pascal. "Are you going in for the Scholarship?" she asked.

"I am", Pascal said.

"Who else is?"

"Just me", Pascal said.

After a moment, Rosaleena took out a pencil and attempted to make it stand up perpendicular on the desk. "What age of a young filla are you?" she asked Pascal, eyes intent on her task.

"I'll be ten in June," Pascal told her

"Hmph", Rosaleena snorted. "I'm only nine past in January." She steadied the pencil, her tongue protruding in resolute concentration from one corner of her mouth. Gingerly, she let go. The pencil stood still. Rosaleena grinned with satisfaction.

She turned to Pascal. "Are you top of the class?" she asked. Pascal gazed at the pencil. "I am", he said. The pencil quivered.

"Don't breathe on it", Rosaleena warned. "Are you top in everything?"

"Well", Pascal replied, his eyes still on the pencil, "most things".

"Hmph", Rosaleena grunted, "I was top in *everything* in Miss Kelly's class".

Then seeing his nervous gaze on the delicately-balanced pencil, her eyes widened with gratification at his meek acquiescence. After a moment, she reached out and with a deft finger flicked the pencil over.

"Are you any good at anything else?" Rosaleena enquired.

"The hundred yards dash", Pascal said, "I usually win it".

Rosaleena stretched languidly. "Ah, sport", she sighed. "No, that wouldn't be my cup of tea".

Master Foley finished writing on the blackboard. "Right, take out your exercise books and get working on those sums there", he ordered. "You've got fifteen minutes".

Rosaleena looked around wearily, tapping her fingers impatiently on the desk. "I can do those in my head", she yawned.

"Quiet at the back", Master Foley bellowed.

Pascal jumped. Rosaleena turned to him and raised a reproving finger to her lips.

Then she bent over her jotter, working briskly. Presently she put her pencil down and lolled back in her seat.

"Finished!" she crowed.

After about twenty minutes, Master Foley announced the results. Nine pupils, including Rosaleena and Pascal, had got all the answers correct. Rosaleena turned to Pascal.

"I came top in that one," she whispered, "Because I finished first".

Pascal found it profoundly annoying that Rosaleena Flanagan thought she was so clever but what was even more annoying was the fact that Rosaleena Flanagan *was* every bit as clever as she thought she was. In the end of term tests she came first in Irish, Arithmetic and Geography. Pascal was second. Pascal came first in History, English and Religious Knowledge. Rosaleena was second.

Pascal's long run at the top of the class was over, thwarted by a girl and she nearly six months younger. It was a bitter blow.

As Master Foley announced the results, Pascal reflected on his setback. His only chance now of restoring some pride and chalking up one more accolade than his brazen rival was to excel on the sports field. With no competition from Rosaleena, the hundred yards dash was as good as his.

But he had not reckoned on Rosaleena Flanagan's fickleness. A few days later, during Library Hour, Rosaleena put her book down and, lazing back in her seat, announced casually: "I'm thinking of going in for the hundred yards".

Pascal sat bolt upright. "What?" he stammered. "What hundred yards?"

Rosaleena looked up at the ceiling. "The hundred yards sprint", she drawled.

"You can't! You can't!" Pascal howled. "You said it wasn't your cup of tea!"

"Oh, I don't know", Rosaleena replied serenely. "I've been watching you running up and down there practising, you and

Sally Dunne. Sure, she nearly beat you yesterday. And her with two left feet! Yes," she mused, "I think I'll have a go myself".

And so it was that a week later, on his tenth birthday, Pascal knew exactly what he would wish for.

Sports Day was held on the 7th of July in Nicky Mulligan's field. The early rain-clouds had drifted away and the sun came out, as did the enthusiastic spectators.

The hundred yards sprint was the second-last event of the day. Seventeen boys and girls gathered at the starting line. Johnny McManus marshalled them into position and gave them their instructions.

"I'll count to three", he explained, "then I'll fire the starting pistol and away you go. Anybody that goes before the gun will be disqualified and the race will start again. Right?"

Yes, they all understood. Yes, everybody was ready.

Johnny raised his arm, the pistol held high. "One... two... THREE", he shouted.

There was no stumbling, no false starts. The contenders took off at speed and charged up the field in a flurry, puffing and panting. The crowd whooped and cheered them on.

After thirty yards, Pascal was just ahead of the field. He lengthened his stride to its full extent, pounding along almost in a daze, focussed on the finishing tape, every sinew straining to almost superhuman effort.

At the half-way mark he glimpsed Rosaleena out of the corner of his eye. She was running like a seasoned athlete, fists pumping up and down, spindly legs striking out at startling speed. Pascal took a deep breath and bounded on, his chest filling almost to bursting, his heart thumping wildly.

He was pulling ahead; Rosaleena was losing ground; only about twenty yards to go. The roar of the crowd was reaching a crescendo. On he flew, the tape was a few yards away. Rosaleena was just behind him. He was going to win. He was nearly there; he was there! He had WON!

He hadn't won.

Sally Dunne appeared out of nowhere. She passed Pascal,

in a blur of flailing arms and legs, storming through, straight over the finishing line, breaching the tape, taking it with her and carrying on for another ten yards before stumbling to a halt, doubled up and gasping for breath.

The great cheer that had surged up for Pascal turned to a collective gasp, then a moment's stunned silence and finally a roar of appreciation for Sally Dunne.

"Sally Dunne, the winner!" shouted Johnny McManus, rushing forward and holding Sally's right hand aloft. "Second, Pascal Davitt, and third, Rosaleena Flanagan!"

Master Foley stepped forward to award the medals.

Pascal played down his disappointment as best he could. Going back to the sidelines to show off his medal, he heard muffled footsteps rushing up behind him on the soft grass. A moment later Rosaleena Flanagan was grabbing his arm, her auburn curls churning wildly about her shoulders, in her hand two green satin ribbons knotted together.

"Pascal Davitt", she boomed, "Come on, we'll go in for the three-legged race!" Pascal, already downcast, protested. He didn't want to do any more running today and, anyway, Sally Dunne and Bridget O'Casey would win that one.

Rosaleena was adamant. "Only if we let them!" she exclaimed. "Come on, give us your ankle", she demanded, bending down and unceremoniously binding his right ankle to her left.

"There", she said, straightening up. "That's us". And flipping his right arm up round her shoulders and slipping her left arm around his waist, she strode out. After a few awkward stumbles Pascal, to his surprise, found himself falling into step beside her.

Their pace and movement duly synchronized, they made for the starting line. The pistol shot rang out and they were away. The straight line of competitors shortly took on a new shape; some edging ahead, others precisely abreast, a few already behind. Pascal and Rosaleena picked up speed, running symbiotically like some strange multi-limbed creature, elegant as a gazelle.

On they sped, past the half-way mark; round several tangled pairs falling over each other; on past Sally Dunne and Bridget O'Casey; up to the tape, through the tape and finishing to a huge roar of delight from the crowd. The throng swarmed round them, as Master Foley came over with the trophies.

The festivities over, the crowd gradually started packing up and making its way homeward. Rosaleena and Pascal sprawled out on the warm grass, their trophies resting between them. Rosaleena broke the silence.

"I'm sorry you didn't win the hundred yards", she said, solemnly.

"Yes", Pascal replied: "I made a wish on my birthday that I'd win it but it didn't come true". Then he added: "I wished for something else as well but now I slightly wish I hadn't".

"Did that one come true?" Rosaleena asked.

"It did", Pascal admitted.

Rosaleena looked puzzled but did not enquire further. "My Mummy has a saying: '*Be careful what you wish for*', she confided, "though I don't exactly know what it means".

"*I do*", Pascal replied.

Rosaleena sat up, deftly fashioned her hair into a bunch on either side and tied a green ribbon on each. Then they picked up their trophies and strolled off together towards the gate.

41

"THERE'S MANY A SLIP. . ."
BY CATHERINE O'CONNOR,
Wicklow

Tom had been in America for over 50 years and had made good but he decided it was time to settle his affairs and look after those at home in his will

In the late Fifties, my great-uncle Tom, aged 70, who lived in New York, decided it was time to put his affairs in order as he felt he wasn't long for this world. A widower since the age of 30, with no children, he was anxious that his considerable life-savings should be distributed equally among his surviving relatives.

Before drawing up his will he wrote to my Granny, his only surviving sibling, and asked her to send him a list of all his nephews and nieces together with their dates of birth.

My Granny, who was 80 at the time, was already doting so the task fell to Aunt Kate, her daughter; who was known in the family as someone who could start a row in an empty room. Seeing it as a way to settle old scores, she deliberately left my Aunty May, her cousin, off the list.

My mother, who was great uncle Tom's godchild, refused to have anything to do with it, telling Aunt Kate plainly that "That aul' fella can keep his money!"

When the list arrived in America, great-uncle Tom, who had left home at the age of 15, working his passage to America as a cabin boy on a ship, remembered the family tendency for falling in and out with each other, and decided that in the interest of justice and fair play he should make a long overdue trip to Ireland.

Without further ado he arrived in our little town which he hadn't seen for almost 50 years. My mother told us children to warn her if we saw "the yank" in our neighbourhood so that she could hide behind the old horsehair sofa in the parlour where he wouldn't see her if he looked through the window.

Having made the acquaintance of all those mentioned on the list, great-uncle Tom realised that his eldest brother's family had not been included. Having ascertained that Aunty May, the last surviving member of that family, was still alive he decided to pay her a visit.

With no idea that he was even in the country, Aunty May, a spinster aged 59, opened the door to her early morning caller believing it to be the milkman. There she stood in her old tea-stained dressing gown, her hair curled up in pipe-cleaners, with two soot-black hands clutching the coal scuttle she had just filled from the coal-hole under the stairs.

Aunty May, whose ability to describe the quotidian was second to none, was soon regaling her uncle with her version of the family history. A natural wit and a born mimic, she was also a highly intelligent individual who had taken over the running of the household at the age of 15 when her mother died from TB.

Great uncle Tom enjoyed himself so much that he invited his niece to dinner at his hotel the following evening, and before he returned to America, he invited her to New York on a six-month all expenses paid holiday. My Aunt Kate was green with envy.

Aunty May, who had never been outside her home town in her life, took up his offer and was soon boarding a ship in Cobh and travelling to New York alone. Six months later she returned home, entertaining us all with her experiences of American life.

"There are no teapots in America" she told us. "When you order a pot of tea they put a little muslin bag containing tea into a cup and pour hot water on top". Aunt Bridget voiced her astonishment by saying "What on earth is the world coming to!"

Two weeks after Aunty May's return, great-uncle Tom re-appeared. Unknown to the family he and Aunty May had arranged to marry, having obtained a dispensation from the pope.

At 7.00 a.m. one morning shortly after his arrival, great-uncle Tom married my Aunty May in the local Catholic Church with a surprised sacristan and a bemused cleaner as witnesses. They had already departed on a tour of Europe before the news reached the family.

The recriminations came fast and furiously and Aunt Kate suddenly found herself in the firing line. "It's all your fault" accused Auntie Margaret. "If her name had been on the list he wouldn't have gone looking for her".

"She only married him to spite us!" was Aunt Kate's defence. Auntie Joan couldn't resist throwing in her "tuppence worth". "Marrying at his age? The old fool, he should be saying his prayers for the next world!".

Great-uncle Tom and Auntie May lived happily together for many years until his death at the age of 86. Auntie May lived on well into her 90's, ending her days in a private nursing home. She was the last of her generation and had outlived all those mentioned on the list 37 years earlier!

HEAVEN'S FISHING BEDS
BY PAT WATERS,
Rathfarnham, Dublin

*Maire and Mairtin are a loving, contented couple; he is a champion
oarsman and makes his living fishing off the island in his currach,
but then came the night of the big storm ...*

Manys the time she waited, keeping vigil by the window.
The boiled potatoes gently simmered on the new
range, brought all the way from Dublin, its purchase
a total surprise, but's that's the way he was. Saved all year, not a
drop of the black stuff touched his lips.

Of course, she knew there was something afoot, but when she
asked him, he just gave that cheeky grin, the one she fell in love
with all those years ago. Then he put his big strong arms around
her and whispered, "You'll see, all in good time".

The silence was broken by the sound of footsteps on the
narrowed cobbled pathway that led to Máirtín Ó Tuairisc's
cottage, home of the finest fisherman on the Island, or so he
told her on a regular basis. His silhouette appeared through the
rapidly fading light, and his movement was unmistakable.

A sigh of relief escaped from the young girl frame of Máire
Ní Chonaill, the same girl who captivated him all those years
ago, when they met at a social gathering on the large Island.

The stress and strain of Island life was reflected in the ageing
lines that adorned the face of this 42 year old woman.

But she had no regrets where Máirtín was concerned. They
were happy together and still got excited by each other's touch.
The fact that no children had blessed their lives had somehow
united them even more.

When his large manly frame filled the cottage doorway,
Máire could not conceal her anxiety as she clung limpet-like to
the man in the wet oil skins. "That's some welcome home", he
laughed. "Sure it was worth coming home just for that". They

both laughed together, until the fish smell from his clothing finally broke the trance.

"Wash up and get some dry clothes on before we eat". She never started without him, regardless of how long he might be delayed. She adhered to a rule, inherited from her mother: "A family that eats together will always be able to share their joys and halve their problems".

On this particular night, Máire felt more than a little uneasy. Earlier, Máirtín had scanned the sky and with an expert eye for weather change, one that had never failed him before, and pronounced, "the weather won't turn for four or five hours. You'd get an awful lot of fishing done in that time."

She remembered her words. "Maybe sit this one out Máirtín. There's always tomorrow". "It could be worse tomorrow", he declared. "Have no fear, I'll be back before you know it". Then he embraced her for the last time and moments later he was out of sight.

"A one man currach," chided the fishermen at the harbour. "Sure it's no more than a toy. You won't be bringing much home in that".

"Now lads" he said, "sure isn't it for your own benefit. With a larger currach, and at the rate I catch fish, I'll have the stocks depleted in no time. There'd be nothing for the rest of you. Sure I couldn't have that on my conscience. Haven't ye all got families to feed. How would it look, God forbid, if I was responsible for another Irish famine.

"And another thing lads, and there's no easy way of saying this, but you're not the most hygienic bunch of fishermen I've ever come across. And apart from that, it's bad enough having to listen to ye whining about the woes of the world when I'm on land, but if I had to hear ye when I'm on the ocean - the one place I can reflect on God's wonderful creation – well, it just doesn't bear thinking about".

"Do you know something O'Tuairisc, there's more bullshit comes out of that mouth of yours than you'd get at the Galway market on fair day". Máirtín smiled, indicating he had won this contest in the war of words. But there was never any malice in their friendly banter.

With the daylight fading, Máire said a silent prayer. All this time the wind was threatening to lift the roof off their humble abode. Finally, unable to contain herself, she wrapped her warmest shawl around her shoulders and headed towards the pier.

For the night that was in it, there seemed an unusually large crowd of people shuffling about, all leaning into a menacing wind with an uneasy balance.

Fellow islanders, aware of her fears, would occasionally reach out and gently squeeze her shoulder or touch her arm. One man encouraged," have no fear Máire. If any man can tame that storm, Mártín can. Sure there's none better".

Six years in a row, he was crowned "King of the Oars" champion of the islands. This fiercely contested competition between all the inhabited Islands off the west coast was the highlight of the sporting calendar. "It's time someone else put his name on the trophy", he announced.

From that day on, he refused to allow his name to go forward and no amount of arguing by any committee would persuade him otherwise. Once he made up his mind to do something, there was no turning.

Nearing the pier, her heart sank. She'd never witnessed such an irate sea, and she'd lived here all her life. Men were struggling to maintain their balance as they endeavoured to secure their crafts. The recently constructed pier, grant aided by one of the governmental departments and built to withstand anything the Atlantic could throw at it, was disappearing and reappearing, as wave after wave mesmerised the onlookers.

On seeing Máire, they halted their activity momentarily, briefly nodding in her direction to acknowledge her presence and show solidarity. She was approached several times and informed, "as soon as it calms, we'll be searching for him, make no mistake about it. We'll keep you informed about what's happening".

Then some of the women appeared and taking her by the arm, guided her towards shelter. "You poor thing, you're soaked right through. Let's get you home. We'll make a cup of tea, or maybe something stronger. You can't do anything here. It's in the hands of God now. That husband of yours has pulled boats from the devil's grasp before. We must remain positive. We'll say a little prayer".

Máire sat, statue like, staring into the flames, while Mary, Eileen and some of the others tried to steer the conversation, anywhere, other than on Máirtín. The women stayed all night providing comfort. Each and every one of them had been in Máire's position at some time in their lives.

And so in the dawn light, Máire and her companions once again made their way down the cobbled track that led to the pier. The wind had abated now and the sea took on a somewhat more subdued demeanour.

The search party had been out already without success. Another was in the process of being organized, with discussions taking place on where the tide would most likely steer a helpless craft.

There was no mistaking the lifeboat as it came into view, breaking the horizon and easing its way towards the crowded pier. Their worst fears were answered, when they noticed the punctured currach in tow.

"It's Máirtín's alright", she heard Pádraigh's voice exclaim, before her world disintegrated, and she collapsed into unconsciousness.

For the next six days, they searched unceasingly for Máirtín's body. For the first few days, Máire clung to the hope that somehow he found shelter in some mystical cave or was washed up alive on one of the smaller uninhabited islands, but as further days came and went, all hope had abandoned her.

Máire also recalled the arguments they had, regarding her insistence that he learn to swim. Máirtín held the old traditional belief that if the currach lost its battle with the Atlantic sea, then better to drown quickly, and there was no persuading him otherwise. "You would not survive any sea that would swamp a currach", he'd say.

When all hope was fading of recovering Máirtín's body, news

broke that a fisherman had been washed up further down the coastline on a beach in Co. Clare. They identified his profession by the clothing he wore.

Although positive identification was proving difficult because of the ravages of the sea on Martin's muscular body, there were two distinguishing items associated with the dead fisherman that would help to reunite him with his people.

One was the St. Christopher medal she bought him all those years ago. She had purchased it at the Knock shrine during one of their few excursions away from the island. Máire was there fulfilling a promise made to her ailing mother, that if anything ever happened to her, she wanted her daughter to visit the holy shrine and have a Mass said for her soul. So six months after her mother's passing, Máire kept her word.

Máirtín as usual, joked about getting Fr. Ó Maoinlaí to say it on the island. "Sure your mother wouldn't know any different. Isn't one Mass as good as another or don't you believe that any more", he teased.

"That's enough," she said, "we're going at the weekend or I'll get my mother to come back and haunt you". Then they both laughed. "You win" he said. "Knock it is".

On that trip she bought the medal for him. Engraved on the back she had the words, "keep him safe for me, always". Allowing herself a brief smile, she thought of the engraver's face, when she handed him the wording. "It's not a book we're writing misses. We can't fit all that on the back of a medal. What if we just put the name of the recipient".

"Can't you just engrave it in smaller writing".

"Maybe I can, but it will cost you a pretty penny and you'll need a magnifying glass to read it". True to his word, the cost of the engraving was a lot more than she'd bargained for.

She had it blessed by the priest in Knock and blessed a second time by Fr. Ó Maoinlaí when they returned to the island. "Is this what they mean when they say, to be sure, to be sure", Máirtín inquired." I'll be the safest man in Ireland. I feel bloody invincible".

"Hey, I wonder will it enhance my love- making?"

49

"Well now, that could do with some improvement, now that you mention it", she retorted. Then Máirtín crinkled up his face in a mock gesture of annoyance.

The second thing was the cable pattern on the fisherman's geansaí (jumper) was definitely of their island, and of their parish. "Make those cables good and strong" he said. "It will bring me good luck and fruitful days at sea". She told him he was lucky she was doing it for him at all.

Yet still, Máire knit and wove with all the love she had for this man of hers. The diamond pattern depicted the small fields of the island. Fields they cleared of stone with their own bare hands, before creating their vegetable patch that was the envy of the Island community. She recalled the many excursions to and from the beach, with their donkey laden down with baskets of seaweed. It enabled them to cultivate the harsh Island soil.

The zig-zag design, running vertically down one side of the geansaí, depicted the Island's western cliff face, that had been battered and shaped by the Atlantic over many thousands of years. "Sure it's a piece of Celtic art", he joked, when she had it finished. He was so proud of it. "This geansaí is like a legacy of our lives. It's how we identify our fellow islanders".

"Are you going to lecture on it or wear it?", she said. Then he chased her 'round the table and Máire became a willing captive, as they embraced with mutual affection. "It will keep you warm and dry, if nothing else", she whispered.

Now the pattern of the parish had brought her poor Máirtín home. She had a spot picked out for him. It faced the Atlantic. It's what he would have wanted.

That year the competitions committee introduced a new trophy for the "King of the Oars" race. They called it the "Máirtín O'Tuairisc" cup, for, where rowing was concerned, he was their king. Máire felt like his queen, when they asked her to present the trophy to the first recipient.

In her mind, she could see Máirtín's face. He would have been so embarrassed. But Máire knew there would have been a motorway of pride running through that heart of his. He didn't take compliments well. It was part of what she loved about him.

She thinks about him often and would like to believe that they will meet again in the next life. It's what she lives in hope of. Just like she knows that this very night he'll row that currach home from Heaven's fishing beds.

BLACK KNIGHT, WHITE CHARGER
BY ELIZABETH WATERHOUSE,
Old Ballinderry, Co. Westmeath

All the excitement of a first ever date in the Summer of 1963, when times were a lot more innocent than nowadays

My first date happened the year I was fifteen. It was 1963, the start of the summer. We had just "sort of begun" to notice that boys existed in a different capacity to the horrid irritating nuisances we knew they really were.

The village boys began to view us as their property. Their way of showing affection varied from playing football round our feet as we tried to walk from school, to dropping the stones into drinking water we were drawing from the well, or tying to strike various parts of our body with catapults from fifty yards away.

We cycled to secondary school eight miles away, on a daily basis.

We all fancied a boy who lived in the cottages close to the school. He was tall, dark and proverbially handsome. We tried all kinds of tricks to get a look at him. One of our methods was to let the air out of tyres so that we could call to his house for a pump.

His mother stared at us in amazement when we called to her door for the fourth time in a fortnight to borrow a pump. "Well" she said "in the name of tarnation what happened this time?"

"Our tyres went down" we said in unison.

"All eight of you!?"

"Sean" she shouted. "Come down here at once and put air in eight lots of girls tyres."

"Bloody heck" he said descending the stairs two at a time, "That must be a record."

We were stunned into silence, totally in awe of him. We stared at him in amazement as he patiently pumped up the tyres, not having the grace to feel shamefaced.

My bike was last. The others were sitting on their saddles like vultures, one leg on the ground watching his every move. He looked up at me from a "down on one knee" position and spoke in a low voice. "Fancy meeting me next week, Lizzie?" he asked awkwardly.

"Oh lord yeah, but it might herald a quick exit from this world when they find out" I whispered.

"Meet me Wednesday around eight at the oak tree at the end of the village".

I nodded, not able to speak.

"Done" he said handing back my bike. Joining the others I was met with a barrage of questions.

"What were youse two whispering?" they said suspiciously.

"I have got a date" I said, unable to contain myself.

"You can't go of course" Mary said. "He belongs to all of us!"

"No way am I not going".

All week I was unbearable, insufferable. I brought his name into every sentence. By Wednesday they were practically blanking me. I didn't care. My black knight was coming. I was under the oak tree at half seven. I'd choked eating my tea. The excitement caused a lump in my throat the size of the Mersey tunnel. Swallowing was out. My mother asked if I was "sickening" for something. Little did she know.

Donning my best attire, and my mother's best nylons and stiletto heeled shoes, I jumped on my bike, telling my mother I was visiting my friend Angela. As I entered the village, lads were hanging round near the church, and I could tell from their unbearable attitude that my lovely friends had been telling tales.

"Has anyone ever seen anyone in their whole life riding a bike in stiletto heels?"

"Not anyone in their right mind anyway."

The laughing went on. "Ya shouldn't be bringing other knights into our Camelot to fight for our women."

"Oh go away," I said. "I belong to myself," as I waited at the oak tree.

I heard the click click of a rickety bike, and over the hill he came on what can only be described as a rust bucket on wheels. No shining armour then. He parked the rust bucket under the tree. We walked hand in hand to the shop to get a quarter of bull's eyes and a quarter of rum and butter sweets. The luxury!

We walked through the graveyard, climbing over the wooden gate and walking barefoot in the luscious grass.

Lying side by side, studying the sky, we planned the long summer holidays, dancing at carnivals, going on bike rides. As the shadows crept over the meadow Sean decided that he'd better go as his bike did not have either front or tail lights.

Stopping several yards before the oak tree, we stared in horror. The bike stood against the tree, completely covered in white gloss paint. There wasn't an inch of rust. Even the saddle, handlebars and pedals were dripping in the stuff. An attached note at the back read "A black knight needs a white charger."

"Mother of God" he muttered. "What happened here?"

"Just the village knights having fun" I said. Then I burst out laughing. Grabbing the tacky handlebars, he threw his leg across the white steed and clickety clacked off into the sunset, paint flying in all directions and romantic dreams being scattered to kingdom come.

Holiday with Granny
By Grace Cowley,
Aghamore, Co. Leitrim

*It was a real honour to be selected to accompany Granny on her
bus tour, and it certainly turned out to be a memorable trip, but not
necessarily for all the right reasons!*

It was the honour of all honours. My grandmother, my
mother's mammy, had invited ME to go on holidays with her.
I, of her 16 grandchildren, had been chosen to accompany
her on a bus tour of Cork. It was thrilling. I was ecstatic.

She would come to regret it.

Granny Butler was known to us as "Travelling Granny" as
she had discovered a great fondness for getting out and about
and seeing the country. Her family was raised and her husband
had passed away and she saw no greater way to spend her
retirement than by going on a journey or planning the next one.
More often than not she would be one of a group of elderly
ladies and gentlemen on a package holiday comprising of guided
tours, day trips and accommodation.

I was her only daughter's eldest child and I think in a vague
way Granny chose me as a substitute for not having had the
ways or the means to take my Mammy on a holiday when she
was a child. Other factors may have been that I was 13; too old
to need much minding and too young to be jaded and cynical
like an older teenager would be on a week away with people
many decades their senior. My cousins were consoled with the
suggestion that maybe it would be someone else's turn next time.

The day dawned bright and clear. Granny collected me with
Uncle Larry in his courier van and we went to Dublin to get the
tour bus from Abbey Street. I had 20 punt – a fortune to me – in my
leather purse on a thong round my neck. Before I knew it we were
on board and on our way on the 5 hour journey to Skibbereen.

The bus was packed with elderly couples. They chatted and

laughed and handed round sandwiches and bags of boiled sweets. Quite a lot of them smoked. The bus was hot and the air fuggy and I felt queasy and I was sure I was going to be sick so I closed my eyes and concentrated on not vomiting in front of the happy holiday makers.

Granny tried making conversation but I pretended to be asleep. I should have explained that I was feeling ill but somehow I thought that faking sleep was more straightforward.

We arrived at the hotel in the evening. We put our bags in our twin room which was on the first floor and accessed by going outdoors onto a balcony which Granny was a bit sniffy about because it reminded her of a chalet in Butlins (Granny would not be caught dead in a holiday camp).

We freshened up and went back inside the hotel for supper and then into the lounge for the cabaret. I didn't know what a 'Cabaret' was and was slightly disappointed to find that it was a guy with a guitar and a mike – I sort of expected a magic act with a woman in spangly tights being sawn in half. When I told Granny, the others at the table laughed indulgently but Granny looked mildly aghast. Women in spangly tights – whether entire or in segments – were not her cup of earl grey.

I remembered that I was rich and offered to go to the bar, my treat. Granny asked for a 7up with ice and lemon. I was not sure what to get – I was thinking beyond the usual red lemonade, something fancy like pineapple juice maybe… or a shandy? Yes, I had tried a shandy recently, which was a soft drink made from orange and lemon, and I really liked it so that's what I ordered at the bar.

The barman asked "Pint or a glass?" so I said "Pint please!" because bigger was better. He put the drinks in front of me. I stared. He said "4 pounds please." I stared more. "I asked for a shandy…" I said, in a very small voice. "That's the way we do shandies round here, half lemonade, half Smithwicks, now do you want it or not?" I was mortified so I handed him the money, waited for the change and took the drinks to our seats.

On the way down, I panicked and worried what my Granny would say at me supping at a big pint of what looked like ale when it was only a shandy. I decided to brazen it out. Maybe Granny knew all about shandies in Cork. Maybe she would be fine with it.

I carefully put the drinks down on the table and sat down and looked at my lap. When I plucked up the courage to look at Granny, she had a quizzical expression on her face. "Who did you get that drink for?" she asked me, eyeing the foamy beverage in front of me.

"I got it for meself, Granny, it's only a shandy; it looks real, though, doesn't it?" I burbled. I'm not joking, the colour drained from her face and her eyes were as round as tenpences.

"For yourself?" she gasped, horrified, especially as our companions were getting more entertainment out of us than what the hotel had provided. They were nudging people who had missed the beginning, pointing at me, the wretched pint and explaining how "Mrs Butler's not best pleased!"

This was too much for Granny. She rose like the wrath of Hades, took the offending pint off the table and marched up to the bar to give the barman a hefty slice of her mind. I sat there, so ashamed, thinking of all the ways this could have been avoided. "I should have got the pineapple juice." I explained to one of the grinning pensioners. "Pineapple juice is harmless." Of course, he thought this was priceless as did everyone he repeated it to.

The next hour passed miserably with Granny giving me the cold shoulder – which was bad – and the rest of the group being falsely jovial to compensate – which was worse, because Granny thought they were on my side which made her maintain the frostiness all the more.

Then the singer said he was taking a break, would anyone like to come up and take the stage? I was the youngest in the room so I think that's what moved people to say "Come on young one, I'm sure you have a lovely voice" "Up you get there, lassie, give us a song" etc. And I thought, "This is a good chance now to put the embarrassment behind us, I know a funny song that Mammy and Daddy like. I'll do it!"

So I went up to the stage, much to the delight of the audience.

I clutched the mike, petrified. But I thought I'd better make a good go of it than stand there, the focus of attention... the sooner I started, the sooner it would be over. So I began to sing "The Rooster."

It's a song about a farm that wasn't doing too well until a rooster, formidable in nature, comes by and gets chickens laying, cows milking, etc. As it turns out the song has not-too-subtle sexual undertones vividly apparent to a bunch of old codgers. To me it was a song that I happened to know all the lyrics to.

Granny made me go to bed after that.

Upstairs in the ensuite, I made sure I washed my face before bed, lathering myself liberally with soap. I was enjoying myself until I turned the tap on to rinse off and nothing came out. Both taps, nothing. There was nothing else for it only to rub the soap off my face with the towel and go to bed.

Little did I know, but there was a water shortage in the town and the water was turned off between 1am and 4am for conservation purposes. I awoke shortly after 4.30am to noise coming from the ensuite. Granny was inside on her hands and knees, mopping the floor with towels as it was sopping wet... I had left the taps on full blast and when the water came back on it flooded the bathroom.

Granny was raging but she didn't blame me as it was an accident. She sent me downstairs before breakfast to inform the receptionist of the mishap.

They already knew.

Our room was just above reception as it happened and they had a bin almost as tall as myself to catch the leak from the ceiling. It was full to the brim. They said they would tidy up the bathroom and leave fresh towels while we were at breakfast.

At breakfast, our gang gave us a friendly welcome and individuals said how much they had enjoyed the previous night. When I let the cat out of the bag about it being me that caused the leak at reception they received the news with great merriment. They called me 'a card altogether' whatever that meant. Granny had a look of staunch forebearance about her but said nothing.

We went back to the room to get ready for a day trip to Clear island. Granny had some trouble flushing the loo so I jumped at the chance to help – it had stuck on me the day before but you just needed to give it a good yank and away it went, working fine. Off we went for a lovely day out.

We came back to the Hotel and the bin full of water was there. Not the same one from that morning, oh no, this was a fresh one they had employed to save them from deluge number 2 – the toilet that wouldn't stop flushing. Our crowd were laughing so hard that I began to have major concerns about their health and well being. I also had serious doubts about their sense of humour – if I heard someone singing Abba's 'Waterloo' at me one more time I was walking home.

The hotel kindly offered us a ground floor room. We accepted graciously.

That night I could not sleep. The room was fine, the bed was comfortable, it was just that, well…. Granny snored. Now, this snore was remarkable. It was not a gentle zzzzz noise such as you may hear from gentle ladies as they doze on a deck chair. This was a nasal building site of sorts, I could hear sawing, jackhammers, drills… I thought I could feel it as well as hear it.

I woke Granny up at one point to ask her to turn over as she was snoring just a teeny bit. She opened one eye and said "I DO NOT snore" and promptly fell back asleep. On her back, snoring to beat the band (literally – there was a wedding on and I couldn't hear the musicians over the noise).

I had a brainwave. Take the bedding into the ensuite and close the door! Genius! Well, it might have worked, had Granny not woke up and caught me. I explained that the snoring was nothing like I had ever heard before in my life, really quite unbelievable, so I was going to sleep in the bathroom.

She commanded me to stay and because she was incredibly angry and insulted, she never slept a wink. I, on the other hand did sleep, but the means really didn't justify the ends. Granny thought I was a liar.

The pair of us was very subdued that morning at breakfast. The two ladies sitting with us were all chat. I wasn't paying attention to a word they said until one of them mentioned being kept awake by some man. Her sister laughed and nudged her in the ribs and said "You better explain yourself, Maggie!"

"Oh!" says Maggie realising how bawdy her comment sounded – you just had to look at the pursed lips on Granny. "Nothing like that!" she said "There was some man SNORING like a train and we couldn't sleep, sure we couldn't Lizzie?" Her sister was nodding so much I thought her head would fall off.

My mind was racing – could this be the evidence I needed to vindicate myself? "Where is your room?" I asked. I think Granny knew where my line of questioning was headed because I felt a gentle kick on my shin. "On the first floor, on the west side,"came the reply. "Oh, that's where we are!" I said excitedly "Didn't I tell you Granny…"

I turned to look at Granny and at the same time as I received a considerably harder kick on my shin. Her face was mortified. "… I was kept awake by the same man." I said, thinking fast "He must be next door to us." Granny visibly exhaled.

The rest of the holiday passed quickly. Before we all parted company in Dublin, I was given bits and scraps of paper from a few of the elderly gentlemen who wanted to have the words of The Rooster for themselves.

I was dropped off home to my Mammy who asked Granny "How did it go?" Granny said "I'll tell you again, I'm not stopping." Mammy and I waved her goodbye until Uncle Larry's van was out of sight. Then Mammy turned to me and said "Well?" I looked at her and said "You know the way cousin Celine thinks she might be going the next time? She's going to kill me. There won't be a next time…"

HIGHLY COMMENDED

FLOTSAM AND JETSAM
BY PATRICIA CARR,
Fanad, Co. Donegal

"Twas in the year of 39
The sky was full o' lead
Hitler was heading for Poland
And Paddy for Holyhead."

"What's the latest, is Hitler going to land?" This burning question was cast over and back around Mickie Bán's fireside. It was 1943 and the war had escalated in Europe. Echoes of the conflict reached us here in neutral Ireland, as we lived with the frightening possibility of a German invasion.

Mickie had an old wireless, so we could pull up to the fire and listen to the war! Every so often the loud and clear reception wafted away in a muddle of noises like hissing rain or steaming kettle, coming back to life when Mickie's fist landed a few strenuous blows on the top and sides. Scratchy bulletins conveyed news of continuing slaughter – on land, on the seas, under the seas and even in the air. There was no end in sight.

Ships were torpedoed daily – as a result of which much wreckage was deposited along our many miles of coastline. The strands of the North Atlantic became a Mecca for retrieving useful and saleable items that were washed ashore. For many, beachcombing became a full time job.

"He's down at the shore looking for "Éadáils", Jack's wife would call to me when she saw me coming over the lane.

"Éadáils" was an Irish word which we associated with profitable findings. Of course not all of the beached articles were of value. However, being the enterprising people that we were, little of the bounty was allowed to go to waste. Jack, Mickie Bán and myself worked "in means", pooling our resources and dividing any meaningful gains equally. We were among the black masses of men, some immersed in the waves, emerging out of the dawn light. Competition for prime places was rife and acquisitions were jealously guarded.

"Diarmuid, Eoin thall anseo," Mickie Bán shouted.

Between us we laboriously hauled a large wooden, water proofed box up off the tide mark. The lid was encrusted with barnacles entangled with dollops of bladder wrack, tightly entwined by a trapped sea rod. The few symbols and words visible through the debris were foreign to us. We could only give a hopeful guess as to what the box contained. A full moon had rolled over the hill. It was late on a March night, so we decided to bury our treasure and retrieve it at first light. In the thin scribble of a flash lamp Jack shoved, Mickie pulled and I heaved until the box was loaded onto Jack's donkey cart.

"Cook, a loooo, a loo."

Mickie's rooster greeting the dawn was all that broke the silence as we unobtrusively arrived home with our precious cargo. Jack and Mickie backed Neddy and the cart into my shed as quickly and quietly as possible. Meanwhile I tip toed into the house and unhooked the hurricane lamp from the side of the dresser. In its sluicing light I coaxed the raked embers of the fire to life, banked it up with dry sods and hung the kettle from the crook. As I crossed the street, I saw Neddy grazing happily in the shadow of the upturned cart. With faces glittering in damp, both men glared at me as I trundled the door of the shed closed.

"What the hell is keeping you, Jerry," Mickie rasped.

"You're as cute as a workhouse rat, you can always skedaddle when the heavy lifting has to be done."

"I stoked the fire and put the kettle on for a drop o' tae." I replied and then added: "Ara, loosen up boys, we're not electing a pope here."

My levity missed the target and hit the wall, and I suppose I could now see why. Lashed with sweat, Jack and Mickie were in a state of agitation. The box, constructed of strong unyielding wood and firmly secured with row upon row of steel nails, was proving a challenge to unhinge. The use of a sledge could render the contents worthless . So, with my small crowbar in hand, I tackled one side, while Mickie and his claw hammer attacked the other. We prised the lid up, inch by painstaking inch, splintering much of it as we went along.

"Heave-ho," Jack shouted.

Then, reeling with relief, he tossed the severed lid to the barn's rafters. The fully lined inside emitted a sweet smell of cedar . We waded through the crackling concertina of heavily waxed red paper which was split into partitions like a biscuit box. The smaller sections were tightly packed with an array of American standard cigarettes. The bottom layer revealed no less than a hundred full sized Havanas.

"I only ever saw cigars that big in the cowboy pictures in McGrory's barn!" I exclaimed.

"Never mind the pictures," Mickie said wisely. "Let us hit the trail with this loot before the town marshal, big Sarah, herself lands!"

We had long since devised a contingency plan for such a find. I climbed onto the half loft and dislodged several loose bricks, making a secret, safe repository for the valuable haul. Jack, perched on the middle rung of the ladder, passed the booty over his head to where I waited to grasp it, piece by piece. Swiftly and wordlessly the barn floor was cleared - the only evidence of our activity was the shattered shredded remains of the box and its tattered packing in an awkward upended heap against the gable wall.

"Ara, leave it till we get the tay," Jack said.

The kettle was singing on the crook, its lid bobbing to the rhythm of the steam. I wet the tea, sliced the homemade scone and put three eggs to boil on the "griosach". Mickie took the bowls from the arm of the dresser and set them out on the table. Meanwhile Jack unravelled a few large cigars, deftly re-rolling them into a more manageable size.

"Now for a decent smoke," he said.

"It won't be easy going back to the Woodbine, after this!" I replied.

Cigars and cigarettes were a rare and lucky strike. In a country hit by rationing, where many resorted to smoking tealeaves, this was a God's send! Our intention was to share the cigarettes with some of our fellow combers, and raise a tidy profit quietly flogging what was left. Still it was imperative that our stash not become public knowledge, as one of those whom we suspected of begrudging us on far lesser successes - Big Sarah - was from our own town land.

All three of us basked in the pleasure we derived from being able to supply a commodity of which our area had been starved, due to the on- going world situation. The novelty wore off, and we joined the dwindling band of hopefuls in their mundane but purposeful beach vigil. So often were we drenched to the skin, the reward for which was no better than a few rough planks of pine. Why had this bountiful ocean turn into a miserly surge almost overnight? Big Sarah, who had her own notion about the goings-on all along, gave it her slant:

"How could it be lucky? Half the men of the country, up to their oxters in the tide, missing Mass on Sunday, over the head of a few auld planks. That carry-on was too good to last!"

Whether Big Sarah's theory held water or not, we will never know. Jack and I were inclined to lend it some credence though on that Summer day when we stood on the strand - alone! The full tide was fanned by a strong breeze. Raising my binoculars seaward, I scanned the turbulent activity of the angry waters. With my practised eye, I spotted a bright yellow object emerging and disappearing again in the fold of the waves.

Jack confirmed my sighting and we both thrashed our way into the swell. I swung my "pull to" – a crude homemade article consisting of a large hook wedged to the end of a rope- in the direction of the yellow blob. I eventually managed to embed the hook and Jack and I began to exert a pull. We then realised that this item was both heavy and bulky and that we might have to abandon the attempt. Jack's tenacity would not allow us to give up, so we continued to jerk, trail and tug. Having given a determined yank, we both staggered backwards at the contents of the yellow oilskins. We had recovered a body!

In the dark and troubled days of the war, this was not an unusual occurrence. Nevertheless, Jack and I were left in a state of deep shock at our grim discovery. We carried the corpse on a door leaf over the sand dunes, where there was no danger of its being swept out to sea again. There we laid it down, being careful to leave any further exploration to the authorities.

"You stay here, Jerry," Jack said, "I'll cycle up to the Post Office and get Katie to ring the Guards."

My vigil was not as lonely as I had feared. Word spread fast and soon the undulating dunes were dotted with concerned neighbours. Big Sarah led them in a quietly murmured Rosary – which sadly would be the only religious aspect of this man's Irish burial.

A small field on the road to Fanad Head, known as "Calvary" was set aside as the resting place of these victims of World War 2 whose remains were washed up on the North Fanad coastline. After we lowered the coffin, Jack and I, under the supervision of a lone Garda, filled the grave. I hesitated in silent prayer as I took in my surroundings.

Here in repose, people from all over the world shared this make shift burial site with local babies who were still born. In keeping with the times, neither was accorded a place in consecrated ground. A few homemade memorial stones, yanked out of the ground and crudely propped up, were all that marked their resting places- souls forgotten before some were ever remembered!

The body which we snatched from the jaws of the ocean was not one of those destined to lie here in obscurity. Important documents, preserved from water damage by the oilskins, yielded vital clues as to his identity. It transpired that this man had been a senior naval officer from a small town in Italy, fifty miles south of Rome.

Through the intervention of the Vatican newspaper his family were traced and they set about the arduous task of having the body repatriated. Jack and I were invited to meet Paulo Roncalli's wife and son. Together we shared in the joy of having a name for this body, which was now being loaded onto a hearse like taxi. Mrs Roncalli walked up to Jack and myself. Clasping both our hands in unison, she said: "Thank you for being part of what has become a triumph over evil."

Her words swirled through my mind as I gazed over the rim of Calvary towards the sea. This sea which had yielded up its dead in raging spates was now tranquil, gently re-shaping the sleeping shingle as it ebbed and flowed. Was this symbolic of things to come? Would the hatred of these brutal times be consumed in waves of reconciliation?

A few years later, the news crackled out of Mickie's wireless, World War 2 was at an end! Our fears of Hitler's incursion were groundless. Flotsam and Jetsam on its previous alluring scale were no more. We hoped that this was a calamitous event the likes of which neither Germany nor the world would ever witness again. Nor did we want to see the recovery of bodies on our coastline on such a scale.

"Calvary's" makeshift graveyard is full and consigned to history. The Lord have mercy on them all.

Memories

THE SHEBEEN
BY KEVIN CONNOLLY,
Belfast

While the whole enterprise may not be strictly legal, there are certain rules and formalities to be observed in the running of a good shebeen

There comes a time in every man's life when he puts his empty glass down on the counter, looks around for someone to serve him and finally in despair mutters to himself "I could run a better pub than this lot". Most people are happy to leave it at that but not my father.

He had owned one pub and managed another and he just couldn't let the opportunity of one last boozer pass him by; nowadays we'd call it a retirement project. Some men dream of their retirement and the long afternoons on the golf course or taking a cruise round the Med but not Dad. He just couldn't stop working 'til working stopped him.

My father had inherited a country shop which did a little business only and he suddenly saw a gap in the market and the opportunity to put his life skills as a farmer, publican and armchair philosopher to good use. He would transform from grocer to spirit-grocer but without any of the tedious legal formalities.

Now running a shebeen sounds easy but it is difficult to do well. First and most importantly you have got to know your customers. What you are looking for is the average customer, not someone who only takes a glass of sherry on Christmas day or, indeed, someone who could drink half a bottle of whiskey and the best part of a crate of beer at one sitting.

Remember, this is your home and you surely don't want it full of rambling drunks; they will drink all your stock and you will have nothing left for your average punter who may take his business elsewhere. They don't teach this stuff at Harvard

Business School.

For my father the ideal customers were farmers and council workers (the men who breast feed the shovel and take a nice long nap in the cab of a big yellow lorry while the rain pours down outside).

Best of all were the retired men (rarely any women), these are the men who will buy a loaf and a litre of milk and buy a half 'un and a bottle of stout as an afterthought. They tend to get up in the morning so their custom is to be encouraged as they won't try to sit you out.

A word on the law: you may think there is no law in the country and many country people would sooner jump in the river than have anything to do with the Guards, PSNI, solicitors or judges. However there are a few benighted individuals out there who delight in setting the police on an honest businessman.

So it is likely that one day a policeman will call at your door; if he's just an average cop he will say "we've had reports" etc. and give you a stern look. But if he's a clever cop he'll wait until there's a sunny day and arrive in his shirtsleeves and announce "is there e'er a chance of a bottle of beer, the drouth is choking me"? The answer to both of them is "no". I can't be clearer about this, a firm but polite "no" will save you a world of trouble and your name in the papers.

I will always remember the day two young Guards called to our 'shop', put their caps on the counter and calmly appraised the rows of empty, grey beer crates my old dad had stacked high against the wall. One of them ordered a Cavan Cola which was suspicious in itself, while the other one, the brains of the outfit, asked my father if he had anything stronger.

My poor dad, a seventy-year old broken down farmer, crippled with arthritis and rheumatism, hardly able to swing a full crate of beer, looked up at them with his cornflower blue eyes and Selotaped glasses and intoned in a mixture of sadness and shock: "we don't sell any of that stuff here". We never heard from them again.

A word on your stock; whiskey should always be a premium whiskey, although a second rate whiskey decanted into an empty premium bottle is acceptable in the cities, just don't try it with any countryman over the age of twenty.

You do not sell brandy. No vodka. Nothing blue or orange or green. No ice. Tins of beer seem like a good idea but need to be kept cold and anyway, the older drinker prefers a bottle as it's just the right size.

They say that competition is the life-blood of trade but the last thing you need is someone stealing your customers or driving your prices down. There should be enough for everyone. Your local licensed premises isn't your competition, it's your wholesaler. They will be only too glad to sell you a few extra crates of beer and a few bottles of whiskey on a regular basis - they are still making a profit on the deal too.

A word on your premises, there should be no jukeboxes, no pool tables, no optics and no high stools. No peanuts or dartboards. There should be no happy hours or anything else that comes between a hard- working man and a quiet drink.

Remember, this is your home but in some ways it's a home from home for your customers. It's where they get to socialize and tell lies and recall the exciting moments of their lives. So, as it's partly their home, make sure it is always clean and warm.

An open fire is preferable to central heating in a shebeen, no matter what people say. A turf fire is ideal with coal added if the priest calls, because it is important the priest feels involved in all aspects of the community and is a blessing on any house he visits and anyway, some of them have been known to buy a drink.

Having said that, there is also a lot to be said for keeping a back-up gas heater for the worst of winter weather, when you are kept busy making hot whiskeys and Irish Coffees.

There is a lot to be said for Irish hospitality but it cannot always be extended in a shebeen, especially to young yahoos who do not yet know their limits, or the drunk driver who must be firmly warned off. There are also those amongst us who could start a fight in an empty house- again, they are to be discouraged if they can't behave.

This is not a "public" house, it is your house and you must

decide who enters under its roof.

In many ways my dad's shebeen (and he never liked the term) was a day care centre for the elderly bachelors and widowers of the surrounding town lands. It got them out of the house every now and then and gave them a renewed interest in life, especially on Fridays - pension day - which was the busiest day of the week.

The customers would start to arrive around eleven o'clock for a leisurely drink before lunch. Throughout the afternoon old codgers in long, black overcoats and peaked caps would appear and soon the kitchen would be full of pipe-smoke and heated conversation.

All the while the old fellow presided from an armchair in the corner rarely raising his eyes from the crossword unless for the latest gossip or to voice his opinion on some current political impasse.

The topics of conversation were what you might expect when Border men of a certain vintage foregather: the winter of sixty-three, the Gunner Brady, how to treat ganders, the right way to sharpen a scythe as well as the dos and don'ts of smuggling and poteen-making, Kerr pinks versus Arran Banners and the usual births, deaths and marriages of the parish.

There were a few old hands who could be relied on for a song or a recitation when they were sufficiently lubricated,

"I'm sitting on the stile, Mary,
Where we sat side by side,
On that bright May morning long ago,
When first you were my bride"

A seasoned performer in full flow could rattle the windows and scare the dog, taking his cap off at the most poignant moments for added effect. If the reciters played it for laughs, the singers expected total silence through the full sixteen verses of 'The Chapel of Swanlinbar' complete with footnotes bemoaning the lack of fighting spirit in the men of a certain town land.

The crack would continue until late afternoon when the party would break up and everyone headed home. The men on bicycles would glide off through the mizzle with their shopping bags swinging from the handlebars, heading for secluded cottages up long, lonely lanes.

Sadly, all good things must come to an end and over time my dad's older customers simply died off and weren't replaced and so the shebeen gradually wound down. This was okay as he was winding down himself. But the shebeen had given him a second wind at the latter end of his life, though I doubt he ever really made a profit on the venture.

In fact you're never going to grow rich from the proceeds of a shebeen; it hardly covered the cost of the old man's cigarettes (Player's Navy Cut, twenty a day and he smoked them like each one was the last he'd ever smoke). But he was rich in other ways, he had a wealth of friends and it's always a good feeling to get one over on the forces of law and order.

THE FINAL GATHERING
By Ena Manning,
Nenagh, Co. Tipperary.

Sean is coming home after a long absence and he is looking forward to the warm and welcoming embrace of his family and his native place

Sean walked firmly up the steep hill. It was early morning, the sun giving glimpses of orange and gold, almost unreal, as if marmalade had been splashed on a canvas. The air was crisp and clear and the whispering wind blew through his unruly auburn hair as it pushed small tufts of clouds across the hills.

He paused for a moment to drink in the intoxicating air, to look with wonder and awe as the cloudy shadows turned to splashes of glorious greens, rich and dew-filled like emeralds in a rare setting. He savoured the good feeling to be here on this bright morning, to hear the birds chirping and calling to each other, to see the smoke spiralling upwards from the houses in the village nestling between the hills as families were starting their daily chores.

He was going home.

His breath caught, blue eyes brimming with unshed tears. The light around his head was almost like a bronze halo circling his strong sensitive face. He drew in great gulps of the invigorating air, savouring the magical moment.

He walked on.

The old ruined castle was still there. The large high gates were rusted and overgrown with ivy but the sunlight dancing on the leaves beckoned him. The small lodge where the old gardener lived when Sean was a boy had fallen in on itself but the chimney breast still stood with the remnants of the stone hobs.

He remembered sitting there, sometimes with the rain spitting down the chimney, or on a clear night he could see the twinkling stars shining through the turf smoke as it wound it's way upwards. Big John, as he was known, always said the Rosary which seemed to go on and on, forgetting sometimes which decade he was on and Sean or one of his pals would say it was the fourth or fifth, with typical boyish irreverence, in order to get it finished more quickly.

Then they would play cards or listen to his stories.

He never failed to enrapture them, his rich voice and twinkling eyes bringing the characters to life for them. Afterwards he would tap his pipe on the hob and reach for the old windy melodeon that hung on a nail near the fire. The vitality of the music would soon have their feet tapping but at times their hearts were touched by the plaintive tunes which struck a tender chord within their breasts.

The boys knew it was time to go home when the old eyes began to close and the music would come slowly to a stop.

If Big John had told them any ghost stories they would race home, feet barely touching the road in case anything eerie was chasing them.

Sean turned into the shaded avenue, memories crowding into his mind, spiralling downwards as if someone had emptied a box of old photographs, glimpses of the past catching his gaze for a moment. Overhead the dappled sunlight flickered through the tree tops making patterns like stained glass on the lush growth beneath his feet.

He wandered to the bank of the stream which rushed and gurgled over the stones, eddying and flowing between the long reeds. He sat for a moment relishing the stillness, the clear water, symbol of life, the peace and tranquillity.

It was here he played with his pals, their laughter echoing as they pushed each other into the water. He remembered his first forbidden smoke and the dreadful nausea afterwards. Climbing trees, Cowboys and Indians, so much happiness.

'If only I realised it then', he thought. This was the special place that he and Eileen came. It was here he asked her to marry him. Eileen, with her dark brown hair and laughing eyes, a warm, tender hearted girl who would love him forever.

He shivered suddenly. 'Someone walking over my grave,' he mused. He retraced his steps out to the silver ribbon of road that would take him home.

At the top of the hill he could see his village. It looked just the same although some of the houses were freshly painted with bright colours. Still, quiet and still. No one about yet. He walked on, a feeling of urgency overcoming him, panic like flutterings invading his chest.

'What's the matter man? You are coming home, they will be glad to see you.'

These thoughts came and went.

Again his mind turned to his younger days as he passed the small school. He remembered the lessons on life he learnt there. Mr. O'Brien had taken such delight in teaching them more than reading writing and arithmetic. He introduced them to the great writers and gave them a thirst to learn more about the world outside their own environment. He expanded their world of knowledge, gently drawing their talents to the forefront of their minds.

All the children brought two sods of turf for the fire and he remembered the itch of chilblains which made writing difficult. Even though he was happy in school, he was first out of the gate in the evening to rush home for a mug of buttermilk and a slice of hot fresh bread with the country butter melting through it. His Mam was great, always there for him. He was the youngest so the rest of his family considered him a bit spoilt. But his Mam always said you can't give a child too much love.

The church looked the same, ageless, timeless. He wondered if it was open so early in the morning. It was. The heavy door creaked as he pushed. Through the glass of the interior he could see the red lamp in front of the altar.

He walked up the aisle. The altar was covered with a pristine embroidered white cloth while spring flowers completed the adornment. A banner proclaiming 'Alleluia Christ is Risen' hung on a pillar Of course, it was Easter! He sat on the front seat remembering his time as an altar boy. He relived again the beautiful service of Benediction, the lovely melodious sound of the Tantum Ergo. He could almost smell the incense and see the bright vestments of the priest.

As he had grown older these things had receded to the back of his mind and somehow got lost in the day to day living and working. He realised suddenly that here was reality, here in this church, in the school, in the village and in his home. The red light flickered, alive, warm, inviting.

He remembered the other red light in his mother's kitchen. When he was small he slept with his brother, Joe, in an alcove in the kitchen near the fireplace. Peering through the curtains the red light was always there, comforting, making him feel secure and loved.

Time to go.

Through the village, past the shop which sold everything - needles, cards, candles, bacon, bread and even wellingtons and boots, meal and all that was necessary for daily life. The pub was still there, where many a song was sung after a match or where people gathered to extol the virtues or the departed after a funeral.

Mrs. O'Rourke's daffodils were waving back and forth, golden yellow in the morning breeze. Peadar Ryan's young lambs were gambolling in his field full of new life. Spring was such a glorious season. The earth asleep all Winter and then slowly the ground softens and buds appear. Primroses find their way through their beds of moss, soft and creamy.

The thought came to him that life is like that. Sometimes we fall asleep for a time, forgetting the good and beautiful things in life, our spirits seem to die but someone or something touches us and we awaken again to new life, a fresh start, like Spring. Feelings which had lain dormant broke through with renewed faith, a chance to begin again, to say he was sorry for his lack of love over the years.

His step quickened and lightened, not too far now. He heard a gentle whinny from a lovely chestnut mare. He approached the fence and placed his face near hers, breathing into her nostrils. They liked that. Her warm breath mingled with his and he recalled another horse he has always wanted to ride, a wild horse which had always eluded him. Wild and free. He patted the mare good-bye and set his face towards home.

What a surprise for his family. They were always asking him to come back. He looked up at the sky and gave expression to his feelings with a great shout of joy, raising his arms as if to embrace all he could see and hear around him.

Mam, Dad, Joe, Denis and his sister May would all be there to greet him.

And Eileen.

His Dad would grab his hand in his calloused ones, raise his bushy eyebrows and give a great bellow of a laugh and his mother would just hold him. Joe and Denis would be awkward about showing their feelings but glad to see their young brother again. 'Welcome home Sean.'

May would make some ironic remark about the prodigal's return but her eyes would show her pleasure at seeing him again.

And Eileen?

Well Eileen would just be there. No need for words, a look would be enough to convey her love and understanding. His heart felt as if it would burst, it couldn't contain the joy he was feeling.

He could see the house now, white and shining in the sun, a blaze of gold on the windows winking and beckoning and his mother's flowers, sweet smelling, opening their petals to the morning dew.

From the open door he could glimpse the red lamp. Here was warmth, comfort, love. What a great gathering this would be – all together to celebrate his homecoming

* * *

The young nurse pulled the sheet over the old man's body. She looked at the name above his bed, Sean Dermody. 'I wonder where he came from? No known address was on his admission form. And no 'next of kin.'. I wonder what's going to happen to him now?" she remarked to her colleague.

She looked wistfully at his few pitiable belongings ... a faded photograph of a lovely dark haired young woman, a broken rosary beads.

'He called me Eileen'. She sighed as she put the photograph and the rosary beads into a brown envelope and sealed it.

WHEN THE MUSIC STOPPED PLAYING
BY MARION RILEY,
Prestwich, Manchester

*It was just an ordinary typical group of houses in a Birmingham
suburb, many of them occupied by Irish people; it was a reflection
of modern, less caring times, until a hard lesson was learned …*

It was just a Close, an ordinary Close of fourteen houses in
a Birmingham suburb, set back from the main road, where
many Irish lived next to East Europeans, Asian and a few
English families. Nothing extraordinary ever happened there.
People went about their daily lives saying hello to those they
met with a smile and a nod. There was nothing else.

The Irish didn't really know each other. The second and third
generations had English accents and some dressed up in green
for St. Patrick's Day. The Irish-born sat next to each other at
Mass and shook each other's hands during the sign of peace. But
if you looked closer at the older ones, the really old ones, you
could see the map of Ireland on their faces. You could see the
yearning still to return 'home." Only nobody ever looked that
close. They were all wrapped up in their own busyness.

At No.4, Mary Kelly's family rushed out the door after their
brief holiday together. "I'll see you all in Ireland" Mary said.
"I've booked a cottage in Rosslare, don't forget now."

"Sorry Mum, I won't be able to come," said her son, "Going
to Greece with my mates."

"Don't count on us either," said her daughter, "we're hoping
to take the kids to Florida."

Mary's children could see she was hurt. They knew how
much store their mother put into going "home". They'd grown
up in a house of memories, of a land they weren't born in.

The bookcases were full of histories on Collins, deValera, and the Easter Rising, together with withered shamrock, used as bookmarks. The piano stool was overflowing with Irish tunes, the walls covered in pictures of Wexford, Connemara, Kerry... with the old record player and countless LP's by the Garryowen Ceili band, The Dubliners and The Fureys , it was like living in the sixties.

They'd grown up too in the religion practised by their parents, who were scandalised and hurt when beliefs were questioned. There were statues of the saints, the Blessed Virgin and the Sacred Heart in almost every room, along with various Papal certificates bestowing blessings on their home, which resembled a shrine.

Mary's son was so enjoying his guilt-free time at university, searching by himself for the meaning of life. Mary's daughter was relieved that this year she and her husband wouldn't have to trail with their children around overgrown cemeteries, looking for relatives they'd never known.

After they'd all fled Mary's cosy nest, the house was silent and empty. She caught the reflection of her tear streaked face in the mirror. What was the point of holding on to tradition when her children and her grandchildren no longer thought of Ireland as "home."

They wanted the excitement of a consumer paradise and cloudless blue skies. She must allow them to pursue their dreams without guilt. After all, her six year old grandson was taking Irish dancing lessons and her grand daughter tentatively playing the fiddle.

Mary had emigrated at fourteen in the fifties with her mother and siblings to join her father, already working in England. She was heartbroken leaving all her friends and grandparents.

The years sped by and now she was the only one left in Birmingham. Her sister had returned on the Safe Home programme and was living in sheltered accommodation near Wexford. She constantly begged Mary to come 'home' to live. But how could she? How could she say goodbye to everything that had become familiar? To friends, children and grandchildren, to the graves of her husband, parents and three brothers.

Carmel at No. 9 took redundancy in 2005 to return to Donegal but she found life in a rural setting too quiet. She missed the buzz of a big city, the theatres, cinemas, and shopping centres. She even missed the Irish Centre, where people sang their melancholic songs, danced their dances and still lived in decades past.

Nowadays she comes and goes whenever the mood takes her. She just can't let go and in a way experiences the best of both worlds.

Two Mayo girls, recent graduates Niamh and Caitlin, rent No. 8. They couldn't find work as teachers in Ireland and so they packed their bags, boarded Ryanair and are now employed in their chosen profession. They're having the time of their lives meeting up with friends from back home, who also have found themselves without a future in Ireland.

They frequent Irish bars and English clubs and rarely, if ever, feel homesick, for they keep in touch with those back home by Skype, Facebook, mobile 'phone and email.

There's a constant coming and going of young people at the weekend from their house. Loud pop music booms out till the early hours and the parties usually end with them spilling out on to the road. The girls wear tiny, skimpy dresses and towering heels even when there's snow on the ground. They seem very alien to the older Irish born, who are often appalled at the language the Irish young ones use nowadays.

At No. 14 lives an old man who every evening, a cig in his mouth, limps with the help of a walking stick to the local pub and then staggers back home. When he falls, which he often does, he resists any help from the neighbours and often tells them to get lost.

His broken down car stands in the driveway with a few

tiles from the roof on top and you can hardly see through his windows, they are so dirty. He plays the accordion beautifully, though, and when the weather is fine a selection of Italian songs, Irish melodies, reels, jigs and hornpipes can often be heard from his back garden.

Due to his reclusive nature, his skeleton like frame and the fact that he resembles Ernest Hemingway, there have been rumours that he is a starving writer. Many think he is a member of an illegal organisation because of his fondness for playing Kevin Barry and God Save Ireland,

Mr. Connor continues to play his accordion all summer long despite pleas from some of the neighbours to stop. But apart from a nurse who comes to bandage his leg, no one else ever visits.

It was late August when the weather was stifling that the music stopped. On the fifth day, Mary met Carmel in the Close, concerned after they'd both knocked on his door and got no reply.

"Do you know he's from Dingle?" said Carmel. "There's a lot of Irish here, where are you from?"

"Wexford, New Ross town" answered Mary "Listen, I'm really worried, it's not like him to stop playing for so long"

"Lets speak to the couple at No.12." suggested Carmel, "maybe they'll know something.

"They're from the north of Ireland, keep themselves to themselves."

"Don't we all" Mary said wryly, "for Irish, we're not a very sociable lot."

Bill and Christine at No. 12 ignored the knocking on their door. They'd come over during the Troubles in the seventies after their only son was shot. All they wanted was a peaceful life. Apart from shopping, attending the local Methodist church and Christine voluntarily giving of her time as a bereavement counsellor, they rarely went out.

Their son had been a member of the UDI and even now they were fearful of further repercussions. They trusted no one, especially the southern Irish by whom they seemed to be surrounded.

A few nights later, after the nurse too had tried to gain admission to Mr. Connor's house, there was a terrible commotion in the Close as several police cars with sirens blaring screeched to a halt.

All Bill and Christine's nightmares were coming back to haunt them, the loud voices, the banging on the door, the people assembling outside.

"I told you, I just knew the man was IRA" Bill said to Christine "How ironic that after all these years, a bloody provisional man is living next door."

The police broke the door down and found Mr. Connor fully dressed, in his bed. He had been dead for over a week. The house was freezing, shabby and it smelt of tobacco and long hours smoking life away.

The police strode through his home, scattering his meagre possessions and searching for written evidence of his next of kin, a will, a letter of last wishes. They found nothing, just old clothes and a photo of Mr. Connor as a young lad, vibrant and full of life, with oh so gentle eyes.

The taps dripped in the bathroom where a faded old dressing gown hung. The accordion lay open and cold next to his body. They found a few hundred pounds in jars and biscuit tins, under the mattress, and even inside the old twin tub washing machine.

"Well, this will go towards his funeral" said one of the police, "and maybe someone will read the poem out. I can't make head or tail of it, think it's in Gaelic."

As Mr Connor's body in a black bag was taken away, English and Asian people in their pyjamas and with bowed heads stood respectfully outside. The shame and guilt of the Irish was palpable. Here, in this ordinary Close, an old Kerry man had died, alone, friendless and shunned.

Nobody had really cared that much to reach his soul hidden by a grumpy façade.

When all enquiries had been exhausted there was no living soul in Ireland or England to claim him. He was one of the forgotten Irish, a farmer's son who had come over to work on the motorways, lived his life in bed sitters, developed an alcohol problem and out of shame never returned home.

Everyone in the Close, including Bill and Christine, attended the Requiem Mass. The Polish turned up with their teenage daughter, for Mr. Connor, unbeknown to the neighbours, had actually made them very welcome when they first arrived. And although in recent years he'd avoided their company, they'd never forgotten the night he'd driven them in his old, battered car to the hospital when their child had appendicitis.

The Mayo girls, who hadn't been to Mass since coming over, brought many of their young friends. One of the lads with the most beautiful of voices, sang *Danny Boy* at the end of the service and read out the poem in Irish.

The young people followed the hearse to the cemetery. As the coffin was lowered to the ground, the same lad who'd sang in the church, played '*Oh the days of the Kerry dancing*' on Mr Connor's treasured accordion. Then he slowly let it sink into the grave.

Afterwards they went back to Mary's house to meet the others gathered there. Many a "*where are you from*" was heard and stories exchanged between the Irish generations on why they had emigrated during different decades. They vowed never again to let their busy lives or their different ages interfere with getting to know and looking out for each other.

"We were like those caught up in the Celtic Tiger madness" said Mary, "we were more interested in ourselves than others."

Yes, it was just a Close, an ordinary Close in a Birmingham suburb with a large percentage of Irish people, living side by side. But nowadays they all greet each other with more than just a smile and a nod.

The retired still tend their gardens and look after their grand children during school holidays. If they get stuck with technical problems on TV's and computers, Caitlin and Niamh's young friends willingly help them And when the loneliness and yearning hits the hearts of the really old ones, they know their compatriots are there to share in their memories .

Bamboozled
By Jimmy Kelly,
Raheny, Dublin

The trials and tribulations of trying to attract the girls in the dancehall days

During our teen years we made no secret of the fact that while fond enough of being in the company of young ladies, the lure of dance bands was what attracted us most. Music makers were criss-crossing the country day and night to entertain enthusiasts in crowded dance halls, but when the big names came to the local parishes we mainly had to concentrate on the music and pretend we had little interest in girls.

Locally, if one were to take a shine to a particular young lady (or the other way round) the news would spread like wildfire. It was for this reason that dance halls at least thirty miles away were considered safe havens.

Frequently I and two male friends slipped away quietly to attend dances in the Astoria Ballroom in Bundoran. The atmosphere there was terrific, the music always first class and the girls attending just stunning; the fellows were probably nice too!

The plus about travelling so far was, well, we avoided the gossips and when dancing was over a lad could usually see an attractive young thing safely to her bike, or if on holidays, to her hotel door. It didn't always work though; one particular night ended in disaster, not just for one of us, but for all three!

Briefly, what caused the calamity was this: I thought I was on the pig's back when an attractive girl agreed I could escort her to her hotel while my friend Vincent made the same contract with her identical twin sister. Meanwhile, buddy Francy danced the night away with another good-looker and made a pact to see her to her car.

Well, were we not on a cloud? And we were, till the dance ended and the house of cards collapsed round us!

Feeling a foot taller as I was preparing to do escort for my girl (as I thought), she approached with a male companion, halted and whispered gently into my ear "Excuse me but I think you have an arrangement with my sister."

My face turned crimson, I felt as if I were hit by a train and chided myself for stupidly waiting at the entrance for the wrong girl. Speedily I regained my composure as 'the right girl' was on her way. Minutes later she appeared escorted by a handsome young man. Taking him to be a brother or cousin I casually joined them.

After about two steps the girl suddenly stopped and whispered (yes, again into my ear) "Excuse me but I think you have an arrangement with my sister." Acting the gentleman I stood aside and let herself and her escort walk on.

On a low wall behind me I bent over laughing and half crying for being thick as a plank stupid, and remembered clearly the master at school telling me there was only sawdust between my ears! Then Vincent came along, the poor lad got stung too but said rejection for him was normal, as indeed it was for all of us!

We discussed what the girls told us and concluded that the line was well rehearsed and probably practised many times on heelballs like ourselves. Meanwhile, friend Francy waiting to escort his girl saw her approach holding hands with a young man. As she walked past she held up her wedding finger on which there was a gold band "Thanks for your kind offer" she said with a big smile " but I am already hitched up to this fellow; he'll do for a while!" What Francy shouted back can't be printed here.

The mood in the Ford van was anything but sombre. Discussing what we should have said and done kept us laughing and awake all the way home. We awarded the twins full marks for making real eejits of us but promised we would give them a wide berth next time they were spotted.

Francy's night out came to a halt when he failed to spot the wedding ring on madam's finger; ours crashed when we followed identical twins leading us up the garden path. Apart from being unable to see too far ahead (and there were few opticians) we were also hampered by inexperience.

Our parents neglected to tutor us on how to behave with women, so we had to learn the hard way! We heard earlier there was a book floating about with the title 'How to Handle Women' but when it did become available it was full of blank pages!

After listening and taking in what Francy had to say about the opposite sex, we decided that everything we learned that night in the Astoria Ballroom would be put down to experience.

"Women," shouted Francy as he steered the van between the ditches on the way home. "Oh Lord could you be up to them? Do you know they can dance rings round us, always have, always will."

But lovely and attractive as the young ladies were who giggled and sniggered behind our backs along with pulling our legs, we still had the last laugh - all three of us got married to far nicer girls!

THE WAKE HOUSE
BY BEN RITCHIE,
Downpatrick, Co. Down

Joe had always spent more time with the Lavery family than he did at home; they treated him as one of their own. Now at Mrs Lavery's wake, Joe felt her loss as much as when his own mother had died …

The cool, summer evening air was a refreshing change to the busy atmosphere within the wake house. The babble of voices and laughter spilled out through the open doorway and windows, dancing down the lane to be lost somewhere among the grass and hedges. The smell of strong tea wafted through the air.

Joe stood at the front door and recalled the big, heavy kitchen table covered with sandwiches, cakes and scones. He had sat at that very table throughout his life. Mrs Lavery had had seven children and had treated Joe as one of her own. He had played with them as a youngster and ran about with them to the dances when they got older. It might have only been a jam sandwich but Joe got the same as her own. As an only child, Joe had loved the hustle and bustle of the large family. Sometimes his own mum had to come down the road to bring him home in the evening.

"I'm sorry, Margaret," she would say, "if he sees a hole in the hedge he's away like an 'oul ewe."

"Not at all Sheila," Mrs Lavery would reply, "sure he's taking no hurt. Besides it's nice to have a well-mannered child around the house." When she said this she would always look in mock despair at her own children.

"Maybe we should adopt him," was a comment often made by old Dessie Lavery who, like his wife, had a heart of gold.

"Not tonight," Joe's mum would always reply. Taking Joe by the hand they'd walk home and he'd tell her about his adventures that day. She'd never fail to be amazed by his exploits. When his dad came to collect Joe he often sat down and had a yarn with

Dessie. Then Sheila would come down looking for the two of them complaining, with a smile, that she had two youngsters to run after. It was a happy time.

Now they were all gone. Mrs Lavery was the last to go and Joe felt her loss as much as when his own mum had died. As he had stood beside her coffin in the back room Joe had shamelessly shed tears among friends and strangers.

"Which one of the sons is he?", he had heard someone ask.

"Oh, he's not a son," was the reply. "That's Joe, a neighbour. Margaret half raised him.

After that Joe made his way out as quickly as possible. He felt that he had to get his head cleared. The front path was bordered with pansies and lupins. She had always loved flowers and often as not she would get the children to weed the beds whenever those "beasties" appeared. Joe decided to go on home, but he only got as far as the gate when he heard his name.

"Joe! Are you just going to go like that?"

He turned round to see Ann. Of all the Laverys she was the one who had always been closest to Joe. They were the same age, had gone through school together and listened to each other's problems through the teenage years.

Joe turned back, a little embarrassed. "I was looking for you, but Sean Brady had you cornered in the kitchen, probably telling you about his new tractor."

She laughed. "Actually, it was the price of cattle."

Joe smiled and before they knew it the distance between them had disappeared and they stood looking at each other. Even in her heels Ann had to look up at Joe.

"She was a wonderful lady, Ann. I'll miss her."

Ann took his hand.

"I know that Joe. She was very fond of you too. You were special to her. There were times I was jealous of the "ewe" from up the road." They both smiled at this childhood memory.

"Joe, let's go to the Veg Seat. I need to get out of the house for a minute."

The Veg Seat was an ancient summer seat located at the bottom of the garden, beside the old vegetable patch. The house's presence faded like the evening light as the two walked down the gravel path.

"Do you remember", asked Joe, "when we were playing Tarzan and Jane in that apple tree, and I fell when I tried to swing between the branches?"

Ann smiled. "Some Tarzan."

They reached the seat and sat down. Memories enveloped them, and they lost themselves in their own thoughts. After a while, with his head in his hands, Joe spoke.

"You know Ann, I feel guilty because I can't remember if I felt this bad when my own mum died." She took his hand.

"Joe, you were lucky to have two mums. It's only natural that you feel the loss. I know you loved your mum. I saw your pain when she died. The down side of having two mums is that you have to experience the loss twice."

Joe looked up. His pained face beginning to relax. They started to exchange stories, filling in the blanks in each other's memory. The ease with which they spoke and laughed was testimony to a friendship forged in good times and in bad.

"This is where you told me that Tony Pearson was two-timing me. Do you remember?

"Yes," replied Joe, looking away, " and you told me to clear off, and that you never wanted to see me again."

"I'm sorry, Joe. I said some awful things to you."

"We were kids, Ann. Forget it." Though Joe had meant to pass it over Ann heard the hurt in his voice. Not really knowing what to say she continued.

"Did you know that the next day mum asked if you were sick because she hadn't seen you all day. And our Paddy, who could never hold his own water, told her everything. Well mum looked at me and said, 'it's well for you Ann to have so many friends that you can afford to throw away a friend like Joe. He's the only one who thinks enough of you to tell you, regardless of what you would think, unlike some others,' and she looked down the table, the way only she could. Then she said, 'As long as I'm in this house that boy will be welcome here, and don't you forget it.' I hated you all the more then because I knew she was right, but I hadn't the sense to admit it."

"She always spoke her mind," said Joe, smiling.

"One thing has always puzzled me, Joe."

"Just one, Ann?", he interrupted in a feigned surprise tone.

She punched him on the arm, half-heartedly. "Just listen, and then we'll see how smart you are. Anyway, the next day Dad was cutting the front hedge and Tony's dad came storming up the road. He stopped with dad and started to shout something and waved his finger in dad's face. By the time I got close enough to hear what was being said all I heard was dad saying, 'I'll sort it out when they come home.'

"Tony's dad said that dad needn't bother. He was going to find the boys and teach them a lesson. Well, quick as a flash dad reached over the hedge and grabbed Tony's dad by the neck. 'I said I'll sort it out,' said dad quietly. 'If you touch any of the boys, and that includes young Joe, you'll have me to deal with.' Dad tossed him away and continued with the clipping as if nothing had happened. When he came in later I was helping mum in the kitchen. I thought I would be smart and asked him what Tony's dad had wanted.

"Ah, he was upset because the boys were in a bit of a fight."

"What did you say,?" I asked.

He winked at me and with a straight face, said, "I told him to leave it with me and to go on home otherwise I'd send your mum out to him. That made him scarper."

Mum wasn't one to let that pass.

"If I'm such a fearsome woman, Dessie Lavery, how come you married me?"

Keeping his face straight dad replied, " It was all those sweet nothings you used to whisper in my ear, darling."

"Don't darling me, you old fool," she said in an angry tone, pushing him out of the kitchen. By the time they got to the back door they both laughing their heads off. I didn't understand at the time, but I realised later on how much they loved each other. Well, later on I found out that the boys had fought Tony because he had started to say things about me. But why did dad make a special mention of you to old Sean Pearson?"

Joe smiled. "I suppose after all these years it doesn't matter."

"What doesn't matter?" asked Ann, her curiosity aroused.

"You have to remember, Ann, that Tony was a couple of years older than us and a big lad. He found out that I had told you about him two-timing you. When he met us he started to swear at me and call me names. There wasn't much I could do but take it. Then he started to say things about you.

"Before I knew what I was doing I was at him, swinging wildly. He would have killed me and the boys knew it, so they jumped in to save me. It was the numbers that saved us all. I made the boys swear that they wouldn't say what happened because I thought you'd hate me all the more for getting them in trouble."

Ann said nothing. Joe began to worry that he had said too much. Then she squeezed his hand and looked into his eyes. "Mum was right. You were and are a true friend, and it's my loss that I haven't always appreciated that."

Then, slowly, an expression of realisation lit up Ann's face. "Joe I've lost count of the number of times my brothers have reminded me of how they fought and suffered for my honour. From doing the dishes when it was their turn to fixing them up on dates with my friends. I've done it all. And now I find out that they were fighting to save you, not me. Joe, I owe you a lot, but my brothers owe me a whole lot more. Come on."

She took him by the arm and headed, determinedly, back towards the house. Paddy, the eldest brother, was standing at the back door with some friends. "Have you no decency, Joe?", he asked amicably. "It's me ma's wake and you're chasing Ann." The group laughed and Joe blushed, which only made them laugh more. Ann smiled sweetly.

"I was just reminding Joe how lucky I am to have brothers like you, Paddy, who fought to defend my good name."

"Tony Pearson," said Paddy straight away. Turning to his friends he said, " He was older and bigger than us but we fought him to teach him a lesson after he wronged our Ann."

Joe tried to catch Paddy's eye to tell him to stop when he was ahead, but Paddy was warming to the tale.

"Ah, what a fight," Paddy went on. "We suffered scrapes, cuts and black eyes. I've no regrets though, even when the old scars ache in the cold. Ann, would you get me a cup of tea, dear? I've an awful thirst." While Paddy was speaking Ann had walked up to him, like a lioness stalking her prey.

"Oh God," thought Joe," we might need another coffin here tonight."

THE END OF THE ROAD
BY MARIE GAHAN,
Greenhills, Dublin

The Old Man and the dog never really saw eye to eye; the dog was his wife's companion. They reached a truce and provided company for each other after his wife died, but both were getting old now ...

The old man sat at the cluttered breakfast table pouring tea from his mug into a saucer. He slurped it down, drops falling onto his shabby pyjama jacket. The room was dirty and heavy with the stench of old age. The curtains were still drawn but a weak sun made a brave attempt to shine in through a gap.

He buttered himself another slice of toast, the dog under the table, watching his every move. Like the old man, he too was nearing the end of the road. His black coat was dull and lifeless. His body was swollen and his eyes were dim. The old man pushed back the mug and saucer and stood up. Then taking the milk bottle, he poured its contents into a dish on the floor by the back door.

'Here boy!' he called. 'Get that into ye.' The dog walked over slowly and began to drink. 'I'd better get this place straightened up a bit if I'm to have an early morning caller,' the old man said aloud.

He moved back and forward to the grimy sink. When the table was cleared, he rubbed the stained plastic cloth with a wet rag until the heavier marks disappeared. Then, satisfied, he returned to the sink and washed and dried the few utensils. He was tired already. Shuffling slowly to the sagging armchair by the fire, he collapsed in its depths. The dog came and sat by his feet.

'Don't look at me like that, Jasper,' he said wearily. 'It's the best thing all round boy. I'm not able to look after ye anymore. Sure I can't look after myself, never mind you, I'm in and out of hospital so much. Then there's the walks ye should be havin'. Since me oul legs gave out, I can't walk from here to the corner.'

As he spoke, the dog's ears stood up listening. The old man suddenly became aware of his unkempt appearance

'I'll have to get dressed,' he said resolutely, reaching for his clothes on the back of the kitchen chair. He gave himself a token wash at the sink. The shirt slipped over his head easily. He had got into the habit of only opening the three top buttons at night. That way, he had less work to do the following morning.

Then puffing and panting, he heaved himself into a worn pair of clown-like trousers – almost as broad as they were long – finally securing them with a thick leather belt. Shoes and stockings were the hardest to manage. If his stomach wasn't so big, he would be able to bend down more easily. But as it was, it got in the way.

Standing up, he put one foot at a time onto the armchair, breathing heavily, veins standing out on his forehead, until each shoe and sock was secured to his liking. God, he felt so tired after all that effort! Then rooting on the mantelpiece, he found the matted comb behind the clock and ran it through his silver hair.

He caught a glimpse of his reflection in the mirror over the fireplace. Did he need a shave? He went closer, stood up on the hearth and peered in, rubbing his cheeks and chin with thumb and forefinger, feeling the stubble. He went to the sideboard to find the razor. It was in its place in the box beside the knives and forks. Bill had bought it for him the last time he'd been home.

'It will make things much handier for you,' he said, noting his father's shaking hand with the safety razor. 'And look, you don't have to worry about dangling flexes or electrocuting yourself either. It runs on batteries. It's simple to use. All you have to do is press this button here and Bob's your uncle!'

It had been a Godsend. The old man took it almost reverently from its box and switched it on, but there was no response. 'Damn, the batteries are gone again,' he said.

He'd no idea how long they had been like that. He didn't seem to remember much these days. Sometimes, he even forgot to get bread for himself and dog food for Jasper. He looked down at the dog before him, who came close and licked his hand. As he replaced the razor in the sideboard drawer, he spotted Annie's photograph beside the radio.

He lifted it up, rubbing his sleeve over the dust in order to see it better. She was smiling as if to say she understood. Would she though? Would she understand about Jasper? After all, he was her dog, not his. He had never wanted him in the first place. Annie had taken him in as a pup and fed and cared for him.

The dog doted on her, following her about the place as she did her daily chores, mute adoration in his eyes. They went to the shops together each day, returning in great form with the few bits and pieces for a meal.

Jasper would go out to the clothes line with her, following her up and down the garden path. He even went to Mass with her on Sundays, sitting quietly in the church porch, waiting patiently until she emerged, and then he'd greet her as if she she'd been away for a month.

There had never been any love lost between himself and the dog. He had always felt that the animal just tolerated him. Sometimes he had felt jealous of the brute. The way Annie spoke to him in soft, coaxing tones; the way she patted his head as he lay at her feet, telling him he was a great fellow. She had never told *him* that. They seemed so easy and content sitting there together by the fire when he got home from the pub at night. The way the dog would growl at him if he raised his voice at her.

All those weeks when Annie was lying in their big double bed in the back room, the dog had taken his up his position at the foot of the stairs like a sentry. He growled at the doctor and any other visitor who called to the house. After all, if he couldn't go upstairs to see her, why should they?

The day they brought her downstairs for the last time and out to the waiting ambulance Jasper had followed the stretcher all the way down the garden path to the gate. She had reached out and patted his head before disappearing from their lives forever.

The old dog had served him well after Annie's death. It was as though her departure had brought about a truce between them;

each one could sense the other's loss. Licking their wounds together by the fire at night had brought them closer. When winter nights were long and visitors few, Jasper had been great company for him and during the day, caring for him made him feel closer to Annie. He imagined her smiling down approvingly as they walked the canal banks on a fine day, or whenever he opened a tin of Master McGrath for him. A knock on the door brought the old man back to the present.

'This must be them.'

He shuffled down the hall to the front door. A young girl stood smiling on the doorstep. She was holding a cage-like contraption.

'Hello Mr Devine, I'm from the NSPCA. You have a dog here for us, is that right?'

'Yes, I have,' the old man hesitated slightly.

'Can I come in?' the girl asked and quickly closed the door behind her. The dog was nowhere to be seen.

'Here boy,' his master called, holding out a biscuit in his hand. 'He was here a minute ago.'

The dog lay under the sagging armchair, his tongue reaching out to the floor, heart thumping and fear in his old eyes. The girl spotted his tail sticking out. She lifted the chair and the dog shrank into the corner. When she went to take his collar off he started to growl and snapped at her as she went to put him into the cage.

'Wouldn't you think he knew,' the old man said, stroking his ears and patting his head. He won't feel anything, will he?'

'Not a thing,' she replied. He'll be given an injection and he'll just go to sleep.'

They walked down the garden path together, the dog snarling through his prison bars, straining to get free, terror in his eyes. The girl put him into the van and quickly snapped the door shut.

'Goodbye Mr Devine,' she said before driving off. 'Take care now.'

The old man stood at the gate, the dog's barks echoing in his ears. He turned towards the path and the silent house, gripping the empty collar in his shaking hands.

BENEDICTION
By Brian Donaghy
Derry

*Recalling the mixture of pride and apprehension that accompanied
his debut as an altar boy in the Long Tower parish church in the
heart of Derry's Bogside*

I am eight years of age, shy and very excited. For some time
Fr McGaughey has been putting a group of us through our
paces in the Long Tower, our historic parish church in the
heart of Derry's Bogside. We are a motley crew - extrovert,
diffident and every personality type in between.

On Sunday we are to make our debuts as altar boys at
Benediction and Fr Willie, ever conscientious, smoothes out our
rough edges with his usual tact. For many years he has been
responsible for preparing the new recruits and he doesn't spare
himself in seeing to it that we are ready for our duties.

"Let's try it this way", he'll say and give his trademark
patient cough. He clasps our hands in his and directs our
fingers heavenwards while leading us in procession out from the
sacristy on to the red-carpeted altar area. Again Fr Willie takes
us through the routine and we'll once more kneel, stand and
process when appropriate. But the practices come to an end and
our big day draws near.

The three most active roles have been allocated. Charlie,
confident even in his ill-fitting soutane, has been appointed
thurifer and will get to swing the sweet-smelling incense
smouldering on its little charcoal bed. Wee Pat will be 'boat',
the name for the incense holder and the altar boy who carries
it. And I will ring the bell when the priest turns towards the
congregation and raises the monstrance containing the Blessed
Sacrament for the blessing.

My father, mother and three brothers are all in the Long
Tower for my special night. Mammy has smoothed my soutane

and surplice and ensured my slippers are in my little attaché case. As ever, she kisses me, puts some holy water on my forehead, says "God bless you" and sees me out the door. I'm full of the moment – jittery, expectant, perspiring.

There is the usual loud chat and wisecracking amongst the boys as we change for our roles on the altar. I'm tense and apprehensive. My shoes and case are placed neatly underneath the form we sit on. I've double checked that the laces on my black slippers, which are the regulation footwear for altar servers, are tightened and my soutane buttons are all secured. Soon, Paddy the sacristan will ring the bell to summon us to come to the priests' sacristy downstairs to settle down and prepare to go on to the altar.

My palms sweat as we process to take our places and kneel in the sanctuary below the candlelit altar with the big gold monstrance in the centre. Fr Maguire, a priest visiting the parish these last few weeks, is officiating at Benediction and that doesn't help ease my anxiety. I've heard his booming voice and he doesn't ever smile. I wish Fr McGaughey was here. But daddy, mammy and Seamus, Willie and our wee John are all in the chapel so I'm not on my own. 'Tantum Ergo Sac-ra-me-en-tum' ...the choir chant is beautiful and Benediction has begun.

With a flourish of his gold cope with the big cross on the back, Fr Maguire stands up and awaits the arrival of the thurible and incense to augment the spoonful the sacristan has earlier filtered unto the charcoal. The incense hisses and the aromatic vapours rise genie-like, and spread, filling my head and nostrils with their magic, as the choir intones O Salutaris Hostia...

I drift into a reverie, lulled by the chant, entrancing and deep, and the following few minutes are lost to me. I remember an arm gabbing the bell, my bell, and shaking it mightily three times. I see Fr Maguire descending from the altar, glowering at me and puckering his mouth very small.

My face burns, my hands sweat and my legs are missing as we return to the sacristy. As Fr Maguire removes the cope, he turns to hand it to the sacristan and our eyes meet ... for a moment. I cannot sustain the connection and lower mine in shame. The priest doesn't speak and I lose myself in the sea of surplices going upstairs to the boys' sacristy.

When I reach home my mother and father are smiling.

"You were great", they tell me, "well done Brian son". I blush with disbelieving embarrassment and as I remove my soutane from the case to hang it in the wardrobe, I devour the smell of incense from the soft, black material. It will never again suffuse me with so much joy.

THE LONGEST DAY
BY AGNES KIMBERLEY,
Port Elizabeth, South Africa

*A tale from the dark side as a young woman tries to pluck up the
courage to do something about the abusive relationship that is
making her life a misery*

Patricia Dowling shivered, edging forward within the queue
of passengers towards the train. She hated this journey
- she was conscious of every antagonising moment as it
brought her nearer and nearer to her destination.

She grimaced, brushing her neat dark hair off her forehead
as she found a seat. The train was filling up quickly. Soon they
were on their way. They had only been travelling a few moments
when suddenly there was the whoosh of brakes, and the train
stopped.

The train had broken down for the third time in a week.
Patricia sat in her seat, staring out the window. The other
passengers began to moan and groan amongst themselves.

"The lines are broken up ahead," one old woman said matter
of factly. "Vandalism I'd say it is. The kids around here have
nothing else to do but throw rubbish on the railway tracks.
Why, only last year a teenager was up in court over vandalising
the line."

Several people nodded their heads in agreement. It happened
all the time. The train from Dublin to Carlow had never run on
time this summer. Some times it never even left the train station.

"It's time the Gardai did something," a tall, thin man said.
"I've got to get home. I'm doing a late night shift at the factory
and I don't want to be late."

It was hot and dusty at the station. The passengers began
climbing off the train. The heat and the infernal wait made
the people irritable and cranky. Many of them had left home
before the sun even rose this morning. It was now late in the

evening. They were eager to get home to their families and begin preparations for their dinner.

Not so Patricia! She felt quite content to sit out her time waiting on the train. For her time was irrelevant. She had no desire to rush home at all. In fact, she'd be more than happy to sit on the train the whole night. Her home was like a prison. She sat motionless in her seat.

She hated going home every night. The only solace she had was escaping from the place she called home. She looked forward to the mornings when she could wake up, and get out of there as quickly as possible. Every evening she developed a knot in her stomach at the thought of going back there.

Relax while she could, time enough for her to arrive home later. She knew she'd have to pay a high price for her lateness but for now she was happy enough to sit. It wasn't very often she could relax. So for now she was going to relish the little bit of freedom she had.

Paul would be sure to be hovering by the kitchen door waiting for her. He'd be grumbling because she was late home again. Well let him moan. It wasn't her fault that the train had broken down. He knew very well that the trains were unpredictable.

"I'm hungry," he usually yelled at her before she could get in the door. "What's kept you?" he'd snarl, knowing very well why she was late.

Well if he was that hungry he could fix himself something to eat. Paul was a tyrant and a bully, and one of the worst kinds at that. He thought the whole world revolved around him. He'd sit there angry and moody waiting for her, instead of getting up and making some food. He wouldn't even take the trouble to boil the kettle to make himself a cup of coffee. He expected Patricia to do every single thing for him.

The passengers were hot and sweaty. Patricia watched them through the window. Some of them scratched around for loose change to buy themselves a soft drink. A cheeky-looking vendor was walking up and down the station selling cold drinks from his cooler box and was getting lots of takers

"For you, young lady," the vendor said through the window.

Patricia handed over her money.

"You are so beautiful but yet there is such sadness in your eyes." She blushed. Patricia couldn't believe that the guy was flirting with her. She had no idea what to say. This had never happened to her before.

"You're lucky you have me," Paul often shouted at her. "Without me who'd take care of you? No man would want you, Patricia. You're just so ugly and useless."

When he acted like that Patricia had a strong urge to laugh at him. When he said she was ugly it used to make her sad, but not any-more. Instead she wanted to say to him, I'm the one who does all the work around here. I wash, clean and cook as well as go to work in Dublin. All you ever do is sit in that armchair all day long and throw your weight around.

The first time she had answered him back he had punched her so hard in the stomach that she had blacked out for several hours.

He hadn't even apologized after, only saying that she had caused him to get angry. He repeatedly told her to stop annoying him. As a result Patricia crept around the house. She only spoke to Paul when he spoke to her first. But still he lost his temper with her, lashing out at odd times when she was least expecting it.

Paul had fallen off the building site he worked on five years ago. He'd never done a tap of work since but that didn't stop him reaching his hand out and giving her a mighty slap across the legs when his dark mood came upon him. Once when she was bent down scrubbing the floor he bellowed obscenities at her and when she dared to answer him back he'd whipped a massive hand across her face. Her left cheek had burned for days and several of her front teeth had become loose.

She had learned the hard way that it was easier to remain quiet but often that wasn't enough for him. He had to unburden his anger some-place and she was easy prey. He towered over her tiny frame. He seemed pleased with the way he could intimidate her.

"Passengers aboard. We're leaving now, " a porter shouted,

breaking through her reverie. A feeling of excitement ran through the crowd. They rushed to get back to their seats. Finally they were going home.

"Are you sure the line is safe?" a nervous old lady asked.

"Oh yes, Missus," the porter assured her. "The line was not damaged at all. It was just some old rubbish strewn about. It's all being picked up now so the line is perfectly safe."

Patricia sat and stared out the window. Once a long time ago she had dreamt of running away. She'd go to London or maybe Manchester or even Birmingham. She'd go anywhere really. She'd even settle for one tiny room of her own, as long as she was far away from Paul's fists and foul mouth.

It was then that she realized the train had stopped. Had they broken down again? No, they were just stopping at Athy to pick up more passengers. In no time at all the train moved on again.

She could just picture Paul sitting in his chair waiting at the door for her to arrive home. He'd probably make a swipe at her for being late home again. Today was Friday, pay day for her. He'd demand that she hand over her wages to him. He'd give her barely enough to buy the groceries they needed plus her train fare to and from work every day.

Patricia felt the money in her bag and clutched it tightly to her chest. She had worked very hard for that money but yet she'd never dreamed of doing anything but what he demanded.

He was a horrible man. He'd made her life miserable from as far back as she could remember. What did she owe him really? What had life in store for her? Work every day and then home again to be mentally and physically abused by this person who called himself a man!

Perhaps it was the face of the cheeky fella as he flirted with her that made her see things clearly. She heaved a huge sigh. She could never leave Paul, or could she? Could she find the strength to break the hold he had on her?

Finally when the train pulled in at the station, Patricia was one of the first passengers off. She rushed up the road, fear causing a knot in her stomach knowing how bad-tempered he'd surely be.

"You're very late," he snarled at her as soon as she got in the door. And not giving her time to explain he added, "I'm near dying of hunger here, whilst you are gallivanting about. Get into the kitchen now and make my dinner."

He made a fist at her but she was too quick for him. She hurried into her bedroom to change out of her outdoor clothes. Just as she closed her bedroom door he shouted, "Haven't you forgotten something?"

He pushed open her door and stood glaring at her. She usually handed over her wages as soon as she arrived home. He extended his hand, waiting for her to hand over her money. She ignored him and closed the door in his face.

"I need to change."

She could hear him yelling at her but she ignored him. Patricia hauled her old battered suitcase out from under her bed. Next she opened her cupboard door and began throwing the few clothes she owned into it.

He was still yelling obscenities at her when she emerged from her bedroom, a suitcase under her arm and her handbag in the other. He was so busy screaming at her for a few moments it didn't register with him what she was holding. When it finally dawned on him he was beside himself with anger.

"Where do you think you are going, Miss? You're mad if you think you can just walk out of here! I'll find you wherever you go."

"I've just become sane, Dad, or step dad should I say. You were never any kind of father to me. You killed my Mum with your rotten temper and hard fists. I'm not waiting around for the same thing to happen to me."

"Just put the suitcase down and we'll work this out, Patricia," he begged her. "I don't know what comes over me. I'll change my ways."

"It's too late for that, Paul," she walked right past him.

For once he was nonplussed. Patricia left the house and hurried up the street in the direction of the train station. It had been a long day and now it was going to be even longer but she didn't care. She smiled all the way to the station, her mind full of plans and ideas. At long last she was free of him!

She wondered if the cheeky vendor would still be at the station but then realised that it didn't matter. Finally she could become her own person. She had a good job and earned a decent salary. Her money would be all hers now. She would take life one step at a time.

Finally she was free! It was a heady feeling. She sensed that everything would work out just fine. And it did!

Short Story

MORGAN'S AWAY

By Clare McCormick,
Curragh, Co. Kildare

*Morgan is getting a bit fed up with the boring routine and living
with his sister, and he has decided to run away, at fifty-nine years of
age! Then fate takes a hand and points to
a way forward for him.*

After a sleepless night Morgan Brett set out with a spring in his step and made his way down the boreen. The sun was just rising over Mackey's hill on that Monday morning in April and the sky looked promising, reflecting his high hopes for a grand dry day. He was finally running away.

Tomorrow morning he would wake in Lawson's B and B and spend the day doing what ever he pleased. He would walk beside the sea, and perhaps go into one of those gaming places where people played the machines. Of course, you needed money for that. He checked his back pocket. Yes it was all there, his 'rainy day money.'

Fifty nine years old and here he was with a schoolboy's enthusiasm for adventure. He smiled. His sister Peggy would not approve ...no doubt she would read him the riot act when he came back, if he came back. Of course he knew he would. Money would only go so far, but a fellow was entitled to a holiday. Walking at a steady pace he checked his watch. Yes, he would be in time to get the nine o' clock bus into Knocknacronn. Then he could amble into Sandy cove.

Since the canning factory closed four years ago he had been fortunate to get the part time job of care-taker in the village school. He had little to complain about, for his younger sister Peggy looked after him well in the family home. How many times had he heard neighbours say what a great organiser Peggy was! She organised him and all his free days, so he didn't have any.

Life had become predictable, boringly depressing. Yes, even he would say he was depressed. He yearned for bygone boyhood days when he accompanied his father and grandfather on fishing trips out beyond the headland. Peggy had no understanding of his discontent. She was happy and fulfilled in her homemaking, having spent years as a domestic science teacher. She had travelled and seen the world, whereas he had never left the family home.

'Brennan on the moor' he hummed and turned his eyes skywards. You could never depend on the forecast. It had given cloudy with showers in the west. He was doing all right only for the twinge in his right foot. Sitting on a boulder by the roadside he took off the offending shoe. His Sunday best shoes were not the most comfortable. He examined the lining and adjusted his sock. A quick glance at his watch made him realise he would need to get a move on to catch the bus. .'Speed walking' that's what all the young ones called it. You would need a bicycle to keep up with them. After a while gasping for breath, he returned to his normal gait. This was freedom, the open road, hedgerows spattering every shade of green, birds taking flight startled from nest construction.

He allowed his mind to wander. Once again he was sitting in the lorry beside his father, he could smell the molasses and could almost reach out and touch him. A squeaking rhythm broke into his reverie; he turned, stepping aside to let a cyclist past. The youth was in a hurry, and had just disappeared around the bend when Morgan spotted the yellow bus on the bottom road. His heart sank. With still half a mile to go now it was too late.

He was strongly considering giving up and returning home when Ned Steel's pick-up truck pulled in beside him. "Hey Morgan you're out early, you heading for Knocknacronn?"

Relieved, Morgan sat into the cab. "I'm heading for Sandy Cove I don't know how I missed the bus," he shouted above the noisy engine. "Well you're in luck" Ned said as he let the clutch out. "I'm headin' there meself to pick up an engine."

Morgan and Ned were old pals from school days. Conversation was sporadic and it seemed no time had passed till Morgan had reached his destination. Ned had done everything except ask

Morgan directly what he was about. The main street in Sandy Cove was deserted as shoppers sheltered from the rain.

"If you're wanting a lift back, be at the Corner Inn at five." Ned waved as Morgan pulled his cap down and set off in the rain. Lawson's B &B was up a laneway on the cliff edge. Mrs Lawson asked for payment in advance and Morgan handed over the money. Strange, how the best room overlooking the bay seemed to have become smaller than he remembered and somehow duller.

He dried himself with the towel, and removed his coat, standing at the bay window. The grey sea was cutting up rough and by the colour of the sky it was not going to brighten up anytime soon. What was there to do? Never one for sitting still he paced about the room and then threw himself on the bed. He sniffed the unfamiliar duvet. The paint on the ceiling was peeling.

He would miss his hot water bottle tonight, and the cup of hot chocolate. Uneasy, he got off the bed and decided to make tea. Long life milk, ugh! No, he could not ask for fresh, not Mrs Lawson anyway. Now if he spotted one of the young ones…

Already he was feeling at a loss as to what he might do. He hadn't planned on rain. All the freedom he could ever want now, and he had to ask himself why or what was he doing here. A fish out of water! Was he out of his mind to take off on a whim when he couldn't make a simple decision.

He felt lost without Peg. She liked to be in control and would never feel at a loss or lonely on any of her I.C.A. trips, and she had lots of women friends. That was it …friends. He never had the need for socialising. Always worked alone as a machine operator in the factory, and refused invitations to the local pub on Friday nights.

He stood looking out the window rattling the loose change in his trouser pocket The rain seemed to have ceased. Without bothering about tea he grabbed his coat and left the building. Walking at a steady pace he made his way down to the strand. Not much had changed. The tide was out and small groups of people walked beside the waterline.

A couple of children were flying a kite. Peggy loved kite flying. He remembered how they had quarrelled on this very spot so much over that eagle kite that he had given it to her in the end. It had been his eleventh birthday present. He found himself wishing she was here to see this magnificent soaring dragon with a long tail.

He watched the display until the children left, then made his way down to the harbour. Ambling along, the wind growing stronger, he counted the moorings. There were over twenty vessels tied up. Not a lot going on. He noticed a strong lump of a lad unloading his catch at the end of the pier.

"Rough out there now," he called.

"Aye, 'tis right enough" the youth answered.

"Want a hand?"

"Sure, I have pulled in a bit more than usual."

Morgan caught the net and between them the bulging catch was landed on the pier When the cargo was loaded into a small red van, Morgan took his leave and headed back up the pier with six plump mackerel for his trouble. A short time later he sat in Macarie's eating fish and chips, nothing like sea air to give one an appetite. "Would you like a bag for those fish?" the proprietor asked seeing the fish on the table.

"Yes, thank you very much," A surprised Morgan answered licking his fingers.

"Is that Mr Brett I've just seen collect his bag?" Mrs Lawson asked the receptionist, Tilda, who was on work experience during her Easter break.

"That was him right enough."

"Did he ask for a refund?"

"No, he never said nothing at all, Mam."

"You're lucky I spotted you there, you look like an auld drowned rat" Ned Steel said throwing open the door of his lorry. "What's that you got there?"

"A half dozen lovely fresh mackerel; would you like a couple for your tae?"

"Shur.. I won't say no, but isn't it a long way to come for a few fish?"

"Well that depends..."

"You're a dark horse right enough," Ned said as his companion settled into the passenger seat.

With a sigh Morgan removed his soaked cap and watched the windscreen wipers beat time back and forth. The sound of the rain and the hum of the engine lulled him into a semi-conscious state. He struggled to stay awake. His eyelids began to droop. He must have dozed for when he opened his eyes, he realised he was almost home. Embarrassed he sat up and cleared his throat. "Did you get your engine?"

"I did, to be sure and it seems a right little motor"

"For the lorry?"

"Not at all ...I've got me a lovely little boat and as soon as I given her a lick of paint I'll be doing a spot of fishing."

"Be gob Ned, that sounds mighty." Morgan smiled his approval. "I always liked the fishing meself."

"Did you now," Ned said clearing his throat. "Well, it might surprise ye to know I intend retiring the lorry for the summer anyway and going into the boat hiring ...with the right partner."

"For the fishing?"

"Aye, for the fishing, and all the tourist day trippers. Tell me now, would ye be interested?" Ned threw an eye in Morgan's direction, saw he was sitting up now. "A fella like you, shur what else would ye be doing when the schools are off."

"Not a lot, right enough," Morgan said scratching his head. "Where would I get money for something like that?"

"Hold your horses man; if you were interested we'd come to some arrangement. You have the time and I have the boat."

"Are ye serious Ned?"

"I was never more serious."

"Shur I'd love that. All that fresh sea air, and surrounded by water. Only, I'm not a great swimmer."

"You can swim?"

"I can, I can, but I wouldn't be planning to ... like."

"I see; that could be a problem, because I can't," Ned said lifting his cap with one hand and scratching his head.

"You never had a go at swimming?"

"No. If the truth be known I was always a bit scared of the water."

"Ah shur there's nothing to it. It's a bit like learning to ride a bike."

"I'm sure it is, but I can't ride a bike either!"

"What would ye be doing planning sailing trips and the like when you can't swim!"

"There you are now, you don't have to be a swimmer to own a boat. Any road, don't the school have a swimming teacher for the kiddies?"

"They do right enough, young Paula Moore."

"Do you think she'd be able to give me lessons …like I'd pay her."

"I don't see why not," Morgan said.

"Not that we'd have a need for swimming, I heard many a fisherman couldn't swim a stroke."

"Is that so?"

"'Tis true; any road we'd have life jackets. It's compulsory now," Ned said as he pulled in to Morgan's gateway.

"Thanks for the lift" Morgan said, handing over two mackerel, "and when you get that boat on the water let me know."

"I will shurly, and you find out from young Moore can she get me swimming." He put a finger to his lips "Not a word."

Morgan's whistling brought the old sheep dog lumbering down the lane to greet him. Peggy put down the basket of turf she was carrying across the yard. "Oh, so you're back and where, might I ask, have you been? Not a word, and me here worrying out of my mind about you!"

"Ach woman, when have I ever not turned up for me dinner?"

"Where in Heaven's name have you been? I want to know." Peggy stood in his path, hands on hips. He knew she would pester him until she got an answer."

"Here," he trust the fish at her, and put his bag on top of the basket of turf and carried it into the kitchen.

"Well, tell me."

"I was . . fishing!"

My Year In Sixth Class

By Thomas Smyth,
Winchester, England

*Recalling the adventures and the plans for a long cycle trip during
the final year in Claremorris National School, Co. Mayo*

Beginning sixth class had been difficult. I was a worried child. The teacher shouted a lot and appeared frightening to me. I disliked that and so hid in the back desks. Other things were happening in my life at home. That worried me too. Now I understand how all those events influenced my early education and experience of Claremorris Boys National School.

My parents were older than my peers, and were subsequently at a different life stage themselves. My father faced employment uncertainty in his late fifties as a travelling salesman, and then unfortunately his health failed.

My mother was a housewife and cared for her brood of eight in a small square house. She also cared for my father until he died, aged 62. Mammy was 55. The older siblings were in their twenties and away working. I was the youngest, and on my own at home with mammy grieving.

Against this unsettled background I became a daydreaming pupil, escaping things. Geography, however, was my favourite subject and one I tuned into. With my eyes closed I could name every island off Ireland's coast. I knew where all the lighthouses were and I still do.

I became fascinated with the Antrim Coast. Pictures of the Giant's Causeway inflamed my passion to see it. The mythology of the two warring giants of Ireland and Scotland excited me. Aged eleven, I knew I wouldn't see it, unless I could get there off my own steam.

At that age I had no concept of miles or distance. All of Ireland looked very small on the geography book page. In comparison, the U.S.S.R was huge and spread the two middle pages of the same book. At my desk I used to place my thumb on Claremorris Co. Mayo and stretch my forefinger upwards and place it smack down on Ballycastle, Co. Antrim. That's doable on a bike, I thought.

I had a bike for going the mile to and from school. A blue Raleigh Triumph Twenty with small wheels and white tyres. I loved that bike, and cycling, except when it rained on me. I'd arrive into school soaked like other lads and fight for a space against a radiator upon which to get warm and dry by pressing against till steam rose from the knees of my trousers.

It bothered me that I'd learned that the climate up north was colder and harsher than in the west, and that if I was going to cycle it I wondered about how I'd deal with that.

As luck would have it I found thrown on the road home the windshield of a Honda 50 motorbike. It was virtually intact and discarded; a trophy for a boy with a wild imagination. I picked it up and strapped it behind my school bag on the back carrier. At home, my mother said I'd get indigestion if I didn't slow down eating, but she didn't understand I'd big plans. How was I going to fix the windshield to the front of my bike and still be able to turn the handlebars? That was the conundrum.

After dinner I went out to solve the problem. It was going to involve no end of duct tape and two straightened wire clothes hangers. If a wire clothes hanger could be used as a car radio antenna, surely it could also double to attach a windshield to a bicycle. That was my reckoning.

The ad-hoc appliance took some fashioning with pliers but I managed to get the motorbike windshield on the bike's handlebars and was still able to turn the front wheel. I must have been two hours making it work.

My mother laughed when I pushed my prototype out of the hayshed to the house backdoor. I told her it had two functions which I thought might silence her laughter and win her approval. First, it would act as a sail and catch the wind when it was to my back; thus, I could go faster. Secondly, it would keep the sheets of rain off me while I was going to the Giant's Causeway.

"Right" she said, and was fairly silent with it.

I got loads of attention the next day at school with my invention. Lads used to love trying out my bike. I also tightened the back brakes in such a way that with the slightest squeeze on the brake you could do a mighty skid on gravel and send stones flying.

All in all I was in with the crowd and lost in the adventure. Needless to say I never did cycle to Co. Antrim, but unknown to myself I became more outgoing and happy. My mother often said it, my last year at National school was my best, and I would agree with her.

AN ILL WIND
BY DEIRDRE MANNING,
Galway city

*A salutary tale of modern Ireland, the land of huge mortgages,
property bubbles and crashes, redundancies, job-seeking, negative
equity and all the rest of the terms constantly in the news*

A lison had the brash confidence of a person who had only
known the good times. "It's just perfect and house prices
never go down," Alison knew she was having no success
convincing her father.

"It's not a mortgage," Mike replied. "It's a life sentence."

"But you and Mum did it. You said yourself that ye lived on
mince for a year."

"Yes, but times were different - mortgages were only for
twenty years. Yours is for thirty."

"We'll have two years debt free before we retire," Alison said
weakly.

"There'll be no spare money. Ye'll be mortgaged to the hilt.
Anything out of the ordinary will be an emergency."

"We'll have some savings, not a lot but enough."

"That very much depends on what life throws at you."

"We have to be optimistic Dad. It's our chance to get on the
property ladder and we hope never to move out of it. It's our
dream home."

"Having a mortgage until you're sixty three is mad." Her
father was adamant. "When all three of ye were in College
together we were able to get another loan using the house
as security. Ye won't have that option if the mortgage isn't
paid."

"Things will improve. You said yourself that after a few years
ye were well able to pay the mortgage."

"Yes, but there was huge inflation in the eighties, despite the
recession."

"But she's right. House prices didn't come down." It was Alison's mother Louise who spoke. "They levelled off for a while but they didn't come down."

Alison flashed her a grateful glance. It wasn't as if they were asking for a loan or anything. They had savings. She was a very ambitious Marketing Executive with a multi-national and her husband, John, was a teacher and significantly more laid back.

"But €465k, it's terrifying," Mike sighed. He had recently retired from a fairly modest position in a Local Authority

"We're not terrified," Alison said.

"Well ye should be! But don't mind me."

"We got them down to €440," Alison said, but he was not impressed. She would have liked his blessing but she wasn't going to get it.

"I'd say we can get you €425,000 - €430,000," the Bank Manager had smiled. "For the purposes of the calculation we consider the higher salaried person as the main earner. In this case that's Alison. Unless you intend giving up work when the baby's born you should have no bother getting the mortgage." He glanced almost imperceptibly at her six month bump.

"There's no chance of that," Alison smiled. The thought hadn't even crossed her mind. They went to the Estate Agent and signed the contract subject to loan approval and paid the deposit.

Every evening while they waited for the mortgage to come through they had driven past the house – just to look at it. It was in such a beautiful location. On the sea road only a few miles from the city it was an old bungalow which had recently been refurbished before the sudden death of the owner.

It was practically ready to walk into, but what appealed to Alison and John most was the garden – a large rocky affair with humps and hollows, a fuchsia hedge, native heathers and a few furze bushes. It was a wild Connemara garden with a stone boundary wall and a picture postcard view of the bay. There was even a small vegetable patch in the only corner where the soil was more than a foot deep.

The house was everything they had ever dreamed of, with four bedrooms - a grand sized family home. They had even decided which room they would use for the nursery.

* * *

The redundancy notice came completely out of the blue. Alison didn't see it coming. She was the senior executive in her Department. While there were rumours of layoffs internationally, she felt sure she was safe. But they made her redundant and retained her less expensive assistant. Initially she was dumbstruck but on the positive side she got a generous redundancy package after nearly eight years service and her redundancy came into effect the week she was to start her maternity leave. The lump sum could pay her share of their enormous mortgage until she got another job. But the bank didn't look at it that way.

"I'm sorry, we did the calculation based on Alison's salary and now that she is unemployed we can't go ahead," the man said. No one in the room was smiling now.

"But we can pay the mortgage out of our savings and my redundancy payment," Alison said not unreasonably.

"For a limited period," the man answered.

"I'll have got a job long before the money runs out."

"That's by no means a foregone conclusion," he said avoiding her gaze.

"What if you based it on John's salary alone," Alison asked though she knew the answer.

"The figures simply wouldn't add up. I'm sorry." He shuffled the papers on his desk to indicate that the conversation was over.

They drove to her parents' house in silence.

"Maybe it's for the best," her father said. He had a look of a man who knew he was right but got no pleasure from it.

"You should concentrate on the positive," her mother said. "You are expecting your first baby. This will be a happy time."

"She's right," John said and Alison gave him a very watery smile. "We may be living in a rented apartment for the rest of our days but we have each other and soon we'll be three."

But they were devastated. How could they ever get a mortgage now? Prices were away above the range of a one income family and Alison couldn't realistically look for work at this stage of her pregnancy. She knew the fact that she had been made redundant in favour of her less expensive colleague didn't augur well for an equally well paid job in the future.

It was June 2008.

John rang the landlord and withdrew their notice of intention to vacate their apartment. He said he was delighted they were staying. It would save him having to find somebody new. But he couldn't carry out any of the repairs they had been requesting for months because times were tough and he had a mortgage to pay.

Emily's christening party was held at her grandparents' house and when Alison's maternity leave was nearing its end she began to look for work. She uploaded her profile on Linked In and her very impressive C.V. on as many employment sites as she could find and went to sign on for unemployment benefit.

"Well you'll be the best dressed and the best educated person on the queue, if that's any consolation to you," her father said with a laugh. He had no experience of unemployment himself and until this his family had also been unaffected by it.

Alison hadn't told anyone, not even John, that she was dreading signing on. Her inner snob had reared her ugly head. She had passed the Social Welfare Office many times in recent months and there was often a queue onto the street. She went into the building pushing Emily in the buggy - relieved that the queue wasn't onto the street on this occasion.

She had looked up the Social Welfare website and had brought all of her documentation with her. She went to a queue that said New Claims and took a numbered ticket, regretting that she had forgotten to bring a magazine. The queue was very long as was the one for Current Claims.

"Would ticket no 213 please go to counter number 9." An English voice came over the public address system. Alison looked at her number. It was 235. She looked around. It was a drab building but clean, with orderly queues leading to fifteen hatches behind each of which was a person processing claims. The queues moved fairly quickly. The place would be an eye opener to her father.

Most of the people signing on looked exactly like herself and her recently redundant colleagues. She may have been up there with the best dressed and best educated but she was one among many. She saw several people in the Current Claims queue that she knew to see, including the man in the bank who had eventually turned them down for the mortgage. Once again he didn't meet her gaze.

After what seemed like an age her number was called. She was dealt with in about ten minutes. The woman said her payment would commence in two weeks but she must nominate a post office at which to collect it.

"I thought you could lodge it straight into my bank account," Alison said hopefully.

"We have had to discontinue that facility with new claims, due to the high level of fraud," the woman said not unsympathetically. Alison swallowed her pride and nominated her local Post Office.

When John got home from work Alison told him about the Welfare Office.

"I was thinking, in case I don't get a job we should try living solely on your salary for the next few months. It will be practice. We can put my Unemployment Benefit in the bank."

"That'll be the end of the Manolo Blahnik sandals and the Victoria Beckham dresses," he said with a grin.

"In case you hadn't noticed, smartipants, I haven't bought anything in that line since I joined the ranks of the unemployed," she smiled back at him. It had dawned on her that their life from now on was going to be very different from the life they envisaged less than twelve months earlier. The Celtic Tiger, like Romantic Ireland, was dead and gone.

"I think your Mum said some famous guy is designing for Dunne's these days so you should be sorted," John said pleased that she seemed to accept the situation.

"So long as I don't have to sell what I have in the wardrobe on Ebay, I'll survive," Alison said and she threw a cushion at him and missed.

After twelve months of unsuccessful job hunting Alison's Job Seekers Benefit expired and she was ineligible for Job Seekers Allowance because it was means tested. She had even tried for jobs well below the level of the job from which she had been made redundant. She sent her C.V., unsolicited, to companies all over the region. Most of them didn't even reply. If it weren't for Emily she would have been beside herself with anxiety.

Eventually she started to do some work as a party planner. It wasn't regular but it was fun. Despite the recession she found that people with jobs were still willing to spend exorbitant amounts on hen parties or baby showers or graduation parties and she enjoyed being part of that.

Alison had come to terms with her enforced exile from the paid workforce and her life in a shabby, expensive, two bed apartment, towards the end of 2011 when somebody told her that her dream home was up for sale again. Emily was three and John had got a Post of Responsibility at the school so they had tentatively started looking at houses. For the first time in the history of the state prices had come down. Alison looked up the Estate Agent's site on line.

"€260,000, open to offers," was what the advertisement said. She could hardly believe what she was seeing so she rang the Estate Agent.

"Why are they selling so soon?" she asked. "They must be in negative equity."

"It didn't sell in 2008," the Agent who was an old school friend said. "When your offer fell through there was no more interest. The family of deceased decided to rent it out for a few years because they got no offers at the price they wanted, but they're reluctant landlords and are not living in Galway so they've decided to sell."

"Is there much interest?" Alison asked.

"A bit," the man replied in a tone which indicated that this was a stock answer.

She put in an offer of €240,000.

When John came home from work Alison told him.

"I think we could get a mortgage, considering we still have our savings and my redundancy," she said. John knew she was right. The bank's website said that one hundred mortgages were being approved every day.

They went to the bank again. A woman called Edel Murphy did the sums. They could get €220k based on John's salary and they had more than the rest in their savings. The mortgage would be for twenty years.

They bought a bottle of champagne in Dunne's on the way to see Alison's parents.

"Well isn't it an ill wind . . ." her father said as they raised their glasses.

MOLLY

BY MAURA O'SULLIVAN,
Tramore, Co. Waterford

Jim was bereft when his lovely Molly was suddenly taken away from him, and Skipper, the dog she loved so much. They both missed her terribly, in their different ways, and were starting to neglect each other ...

The shopping bag hung limply on the kitchen door. Jim gazed at it as though in a trance. Its creases seemed to take on a sad expression matching his mood. It's most recent load lay on the kitchen table, bread, beans, tea and dog food. The room was silent except for the ticking of a clock.

An unwelcome autumn chill had crept into the small kitchen making Jim shiver. He pulled his dressing gown tighter round him but refrained from switching on the heating. The cold seemed more honest to him than the pseudo warmth from the radiator. He noticed the light fading as he looked out the window and could just make out the garden bench.

The unkempt, unweeded garden neatened by the twilight, looked almost as it did forty years ago. So many photographs carefully framed throughout the house, captured good times with smiling people sitting on that bench. He remembered the day they first got it. She was childlike in her excitement. She sat and admired its arching shape and its workmanship. He remembered vividly her smiling face.

Oh that smile, he missed it so much. He closed his eyes and could feel the warmth and love it generated. Such a long time ago, so much had changed, only the bench though somewhat neglected, looked anything like it did on that day. He had changed, the world had changed.

He stood up, stretched his aching back and moved slowly to turn on the light. He was dazzled momentarily by the brightness. When he recovered, his eyes met one of those happy photographs from long ago. He couldn't remember who had taken the shot but Molly, himself and Patch, their first dog, radiated happiness as they sat in the garden.

He contemplated making tea but decided it was too much trouble. The bottle of whisky at the back of the press would be more appropriate but he was never really a drinker. A glass of water would do. He opened and retied the belt of his dressing gown. It was looking pretty grubby and getting on like himself. It must be fifteen years old now.

He remembered when Molly gave it to him with a pair of slippers when he retired from the factory. She said he would need them for his new life of leisure. He was glad to leave the factory. The work was long and hard and more suitable to a younger man. Many of his workmates dreaded the thought of retirement but Jim looked forward to spending more time at home with Molly.

He had enjoyed those last years with her as much as their first. They would start the day by bringing Skipper for a walk. He had strayed into their garden one day and never left. Molly had tried to find the owner but failed. He was a black and white Border collie. They had many dogs over the years but Skipper was to be Molly's last.

She adored all animals and not having had any children they benefited from her maternal instinct and were showered with love and attention. Skipper spent all his time following Molly around. He would plank himself at her feet watching her every move as she cooked dinner or made some of those lovely scones. Jim missed that homely smell of baking in the kitchen.

Skipper had spent weeks searching for Molly around the house. Each time someone came to the door he expected it to be her but was disappointed each time. Eventually Skipper no longer liked coming into the house. He took to staying outside or in the kennel. Jim hardly knew he was there. He was an old dog now and, like Jim, suffered from aches and pains but he refused to come indoors. He too was unhappy in a world without her.

Molly was always fit and healthy, encouraging Jim to take more exercise, especially after his retirement. She worried about his weight and cholesterol. The last thing either of them expected was for Molly to become ill. She returned one day from her doctor and Jim knew immediately something was wrong. A routine blood test had highlighted an abnormality and she was to be admitted to hospital to undergo further tests.

Jim's heart raced even now as he thought about the panic that ran through his veins. It was Molly who tried to make him relax, arranging things and ensuring that all would run smoothly at home while she was in hospital. The consultant didn't pull any punches. It was a tumour, it was very serious but it was operable.

They were both in shock but Molly as usual was positive in her outlook. She was delighted that the operation was scheduled for the following day. "Let's get this over with "she said as she signed the necessary paperwork. Jim held her hand as they wheeled her to the operating area. She was still smiling and reminding him to get some rest and see to Skipper.

He told her he would be there when she came round. He didn't go home but paced up and down until at last, the surgeon came through the door. "I'm so sorry Mr Phelan, we did everything we could but the tumour had become embedded ..." The use left his legs and he heard no more.

Molly had been a very popular lady in the neighbourhood, involved in many local activities. This was reflected in the crowded church on the day of her funeral. Countless people came up to Jim to say how wonderful she was and how much they would all miss her. Later that day neighbour after neighbour called to the house to sit with him for a while.

He was glad when they all eventually left. He was worn out shaking hands and being polite. He knew they meant well but he somehow resented the fact that after they had poured out their sympathy they would go back to their normal lives. His would never be normal again.

Four months had passed since that day, four miserable months. He felt numb, he had not been able to cry even during those long lonely nights. The beautiful summer weather gave him no pleasure. Happiness was only found when his thoughts were lost in long ago, but then cold reality returned like a knife piercing his heart.

His health had deteriorated without Molly's encouragement and guidance. Evidence of this lay in the array of medications before him on the table. The doctor had prescribed for his high blood pressure, depression, arthritic pain and sleeplessness. He had wanted him to attend bereavement counselling but Jim had no wish to talk to a stranger about his innermost thoughts. Anyway, no one could bring Molly back, so what was the point.

Jim longed to have a firm belief in the afterlife. He was a practising Catholic and still attended first mass on Sundays. It was quiet at that hour, not too many people asking him how he was. He went out of habit, condition, culture but not because he believed. He had tried to convince himself that Molly would be in a heavenly place waiting for him when his time came but as much as he wanted to believe, he wasn't convinced. He still prayed for her soul in case he was wrong.

He looked at the brown bottle containing the sleeping tablets; how many would it take he wondered. He opened the lid and tipped them out onto the table. He slowly stood and with aching back looked for the photo album in the press behind him. With great effort he lifted the heavy book on to the table and pushed away two day's unwashed dishes. He would take one last walk through their wonderful time together.

The first image was of a young smiling Molly, her magnificent auburn hair blowing in the wind. This one was taken just before they met so she would have been just eighteen at that time. The next page had shots of them in their early courtship days. He remembered the first time he saw her at a local dance. She was on holidays, staying at her cousin's house nearby. He was awe struck and couldn't find the nerve to ask her to dance. Afterwards he kicked himself for being such a coward.

He admired her from afar over the following week. Then he found out she was going home on Sunday so he knew that the next Saturday night's dance would be his only chance. He was still nervous when the band started to play. Then he noticed another boy heading in her direction. So, without further thought he quickly made his way to her and asked her to dance.

Looking back he wondered why he had been so nervous. I suppose she was so breathtakingly beautiful he thought she might laugh at him. She didn't laugh but she did smile as she started to dance with him. Within a few minutes he knew her name and where she was from. He also knew that he had to find a way to see this girl again. He asked if he could write to her and she said she'd like that.

The letters went back and forth over the next few months and at Christmas she came to stay with her cousins again. They had great fun together and when it was time to part they both knew that they wanted to spend the rest of their lives together. He applied for a job near her home and within two years they were married. They had looked forward to having a family but that never happened. Molly in particular was disappointed but they came to accept it.

As Jim turned another page he admired his beautiful wife in her wedding gown. He was so proud that day and they were both full of plans for their future. He went through the album lost in thought until eventually he found himself on the last page. This had a photograph of Molly and Skipper looking adoringly at each other.

Poor Skipper, he hadn't been fed for two days. He'd better fill his dish and leave some water for him. He closed the album and reached for the tin of dog food. As he approached the kennel Skipper came slowly out to meet him his tail gently wagging. Jim spooned the food into his dish and turned to go back into the house. Skipper, leaving the food, followed Jim.

He turned and patted the dog's head and felt how cold he was and noticed how thin he had become. "It's got a bit colder out here now hasn't it Skipper?" At the sound of his voice Skipper's tail wagged furiously and suddenly Jim felt an overwhelming pity for him. He bent down and rubbed the dog as tears started to well up in his eyes. "Oh Skipper I know, you miss her too, you poor dog".

Skipper responded by licking Jim's face. Suddenly, the dam broke and tears started to pour down Jim's face. "You're the only one who really understands", he said to the dog. As he sniffed and wiped away the tears which were still falling, he picked up the dish and carried it into the kitchen.

"Come on Skipper, come inside, it's too cold out there for an old dog now, you have to eat something. What would Molly say if she saw the state of you?" Skipper slowly followed Jim inside, "That's a good dog we'll have to fatten you up a bit. Maybe I'll go as far as the pet shop tomorrow and buy the food that Molly used to give you. You're still so cold, let's get some heat going here and make you nice and comfortable. We too old codgers will have to look after each other now."

A Day With My Great Aunt Biddy
By Anne McCormack,
Enniscorthy, Co. Wexford

“ My God she's big” whispered Mary.
"She's not wearing any shoes either" giggled Jane.
"Shut up you two, this is my great aunt Biddy"
I was annoyed with my two friends, afraid my aunt would hear their comments. My mother often asked me to take some supplies to Biddy during the summer. As this was a lovely day, I had asked my friends to accompany me on the three mile walk. I was beginning to have second thoughts already.

Biddy had met us girls with the words, "If I'd known you were coming, I'd have killed something."

She greeted most visitors with these words. Mary and Jane were not quite sure what she had in mind. However, they could certainly believe what she said, looking at the stature of this woman before them.

Great Aunt Biddy lived alone in a white-washed thatched cottage, which stood in the boggy towns land of Corcar on a mountain road in South West Donegal. In winter it was a desolate, windswept, marshy spot while in summer something magical happened.

Purple heather, the yellow furze, which the locals called 'whins', and the bog cotton grew abundantly, changing this isolated locality from dangerous and threatening into something magical and alluring.

"Tar isteach, tar isteach, come in children. Don't mind me. I'm an old mountain woman. You will have some tea and cake, or milk if you wish. Come on inside, I'm delighted to see you. I don't get many visitors up here you know.

"It can get lonely at times."

Her excitement at seeing us was real. She had in fact spotted three girls coming down the 'bealach bui' once we came over the brow of the small hill.

"Tea would be lovely Aunt Biddy." Mary and Jane just nodded in agreement.

The cottage itself was small, the front door opened straight into the main room, which served as parlour and kitchen. On one wall was a large open fireplace with hooks for pots. A Welsh dresser was bedecked with speckled crockery. The plates shone in the sunlight that streamed in through a tiny window. A beautiful ornate Tilly lamp stood on a small table in a corner by the fireplace.

At the opposite end of this room was a door which led into the bedroom. A back door opened to reveal a small hallway. A chair here held a galvanised bath, washboard and red carbolic soap. From this hallway you could step into a garden.

A chicken run containing a dozen or more chickens was visible here. Ducks ambled around on the grass and a cow was grazing in a small field. There was a donkey in a small lean-to and a trap was standing by the side of the cottage.

"Which one of these would have been murdered" whispered Jane. I knew just what Biddy was like and I had to hide my face from the girls. My aunt was busy inside all this time, singing and bustling around getting things ready for tea. When we came in again, she was carrying on a running commentary on what she was making.

"Add to flour, eggs, buttermilk some cut apples and blend into a cake. Place in that pot on the hook over the fire and then wait patiently. All you really need girls are a few basics and you can entertain the Lord himself ". I loved the simplicity of Biddy's ways.

We watched my aunt as she went about her chores. She was a large woman, six foot of muscle and strength. Her unruly black hair was done up in a bun at the back of her neck. In summer, Biddy never wore shoes, unless going to Mass or Glenties for supplies. She had lived in this place all her life, leaving school aged twelve years, following the death of her father.

She managed this small holding with her mother until she too passed away. Biddy had never married. No one had ever questioned this and Biddy, being a strong willed woman, would not have appreciated their prying.

"Come on girls, sit in to the table, tea is ready".

Mary and Jane's next surprise came in the shape of what they were going to drink the tea from. Biddy seeing the looks on their faces could not resist having her fun.

"Yes Jane, these do look like sugar bowls. You are in the mountains now and that's what we drink tea from up here. It's always strange when people from the town come up here for the first time".

Tea was certainly worth waiting for that day and the apple bread, or cake or whatever Biddy had called it, was delicious. We washed and tidied up after tea and my friends seemed genuinely sorry to leave. The long walk down the mountain road went by all too quickly. It had been a most enjoyable summer's day.

Sad to say, Biddy is no longer with us. She has gone to her eternal reward. The little cottage is now in ruins. The countryside is poorer for the loss of characters like my Great Aunt Biddy. When guests call on me unexpectedly, I sometimes find myself using Biddy's words,

"If I'd known you were coming, I'd have killed something".

Short Story

ALL ON A SUMMER'S DAY

BY MAE LEONARD,

Naas, Co. Kildare

*An old lady in America remembers her happy Clare childhood,
that was suddenly torn apart on a day in 1888 by the terror of the
landlord's battering ram as the whole family are evicted and thrown
out on the side of the road …*

Sometimes, in my dreams, I touch the wall. I trace the shape
of the stones with my fingertips. I smell the dampness of
the mortar holding everything together. I chase away the
clucking brown hens cluttering the doorway. I push open the
cabin door to smell the fresh straw, the sods of dry brown turf
stored there and the milky scent of a suckling calf. I hear the
slow steady breathing of mother cow and the piping of small
turkeys.

I make my way around to the haggard at the back and I
smile wryly reminding myself of the hissing gander and the bad
tempered cockerel who often drew blood when he pecked me.

Look! A startled woodpigeon coos a warning and flutters
frantically out the glassless back window as I peer into the
darkness of the stable. This was once the house, our house, the
house of my people, my parents, my sisters and brothers, my
family. All gone now; there's only me, me to remember and me
to remind those who might forget or those who would turn their
heads away.

Look at me in my old age. I am alone, wrinkled and feeble but
I want none of your pity. Alone I may be but I have my prayers,
my books and a wealth of memories. Here in Atlanta, Georgia,
now, I want to go back home. I yearn to go back to the place
where I was born. In all these years I have never returned to the
ould sod. I could not look upon that old derelict, the house, the
farm; after all we went through to save it.

I could never face it. The sentiment would kill me. Now it

133

is time. Take my hand, please, please. Come back home with me to West Clare, to Carradotia near Killimer where the new ferryboat takes you across the Shannon to County Kerry.

Let me tell you what happened in July 1888 ...
It is a glorious summer's day, thank God. Feel the heat rising from the salty water warmed by the Gulf Stream. Smell the iodine in the blistered seaweed. A school of dolphin ripples the smooth water. The warmth of the sun intensifies the perfume of the honeysuckle to mingle with that of the meadow sweet growing along the edge of the boreen leading up Carradotia Hill. Everything seems to be well with the world.

This is the small farm of the Connell family, my family. Michael Connell - that's my father - sitting there on the low wall in front of the old homestead, smoking his pipe. My mother sits beside him rocking a tiny baby in her arms; this is the youngest of their six children - the other five, including myself, are within the house.

Dada's hands are trembling and there's a terrible fear in Mamma's eyes. No wonder the baby is unsettled, my Mama is transferring her feelings without even realising it. She breathes in and out at a rapid rate, her heart thumping wildly. She holds the baby tightly, too tightly, to her and that brings forth a mighty howl from the little rosebud mouth.

"Wisha, wisha can't you be quiet, alanna." She coaxes the baby into sleep with soothing sounds. "Codail a leanbh le cronan na mbeach. " She sings softly. "Sleep little baby with the humming of bees" The beautiful sound of the Gaelic words lilt in lullaby. And it works. The baby settles and sleeps.

Seconds later there is an almighty screech as a murder of black crows, startled from the high trees on the low road, caw a warning against the pure blue of the sky and the cry goes up – "They're coming."

The sun glints now on the helmets of the huge force of militia – a procession three miles long - marching out from the town of Kilrush. It winds along the shore road where the upturned tarred currachs await the next salmon fishing. Crunch-crunch-crunch the soldiers' stout boots beat in unison on the sandy road. Brass buttons twinkle in the sunshine to mock the fearsome occasion. The water laps with only the tiniest sigh onto the rocky beach.

Our time has come.

We are to be evicted by order of the Landlord – Vandeleur. This is the culmination of a whole year of negotiation because of the ever-increasing rents inflicted on Ireland's tenant farmers by absentee landlords who want to clear them off the land in order to graze their own cattle. In our case the land is to be divided and sold off because the landlord is no longer interested in running his property. And he has no feelings for the land and less for us. We are just a thorn in his side.

Twenty seven tenant farmers and families are to be swept off the land for Vandeleur's pleasure. Michael Davitt, God bless him, the tenant farmers' hero politician, came to West Clare urging the farmers to follow the plan of campaign drawn up by the National Land League.

A fair rent was collected from each farm by the committee and paid into a bank account and kept there to be handed over when terms are finally agreed. But nothing has been agreed. The landlord's agent is severe and resolute in the execution of his master's orders. The tenant farmers must pay the exorbitant rent or get off his land, be evicted.

Eviction! The very word strikes terror into every man, woman and child in our part of County Clare. And this after having weathered the storm of the Great Famine, and the bad weather that diseased the corn two summers in a row, and survived to a full harvest this summer of our Lord 1888.

My Dada often told the story of how in December two years previously all the two hundred Vandeleur tenants came together in Kilrush. They appointed representatives to meet Vandeleur's agent, Mr. Studdart, to discuss a reduction of rent. It was refused. There were other proposals and negotiations that went on for over a year with no favourable results. The landlord stood resolute - pay or be evicted was his reply. He prepared himself for the worst.

Thus, a large force of police arrived in Kilrush, possibly to frighten the tenant farmers into paying the exorbitant rents but failing compliance, to assist in the evictions. Vandeleur's agent met with the tenants several times in an effort to reach agreement. There was none.

At the beginning of July 1888 troops were sent to Kilrush. Huzzars, Sherwood Foresters and Royal Berkshires moved into the grounds of the Vandeleur mansion. On the 18th of July three families were evicted. Then we knew it was the turn of the Connells of Carradotia. Us.

How do you prepare for an eviction? Our poor misfortunate Dada, Michael Connell, does his best.

Kind neighbours share between them the responsibility of our livestock until things can be put right again. Stocks of food have been donated and stored elsewhere. Small as we children are, we play our part too. We are given our instructions.

Under the cover of darkness last night Dada and some of the local men dug a wide gully in the narrow road leading to the house hoping to, at least, delay the fateful moment. When the soldiers reach it they are halted for a short while. Some manage to scramble over but that dreaded weapon, the battering ram, has to be dismantled and carried across bit by bit.

The gathered crowd jeers at the halted army and officials as the heavy equipment is moved further in the road and put together again, only to face another obstacle further in the road, another gully.

But it is only a matter of time before Captain Croker, the Sheriff, arrives at our front door on Carradotia Hill, Killimer, and formally demands possession of the house and lands. Dada sits outside seemingly impassive. He says nothing. Mamma bites her lip in worry lest she betray him by begging or even crying for mercy. Even the baby seems to be holding his breath.

As the sheriff approaches the door we lift the big pot of hot stirabout (porridge) and throw the contents out the side window at the sheriff. Scalded, spluttering and shaking his fist he shouts "I warn those people that the house will be fired into if there is any more of that."

Dada remains seated on the wall with Mama and the baby. We, inside the house, put up a brave fight and scald the sheriff again with boiling water. He is outraged.

He orders the soldiers to climb onto the thatched roof and stuff the chimney with wet straw to smoke us out of the house. We hear the battering ram put into position and aimed at a weak spot in the front wall. One thud sends a heap of loose stones toppling inwards. We scream with fright. Another thud against the wall and it seems as if the roof will cave in. We scream and scream and scream.

Poor Dada can take no more and he approaches the sheriff. We hear him beg for the childer to be allowed out. Permission is granted. The five of us crawl out through the breach, coughing and gasping for air. The house is taken over by civic officials and our few sticks of furniture flung out onto the road.

Oh yes, I remember it well.

Twenty-one other families on the Vandeleur Estate are evicted over the next couple of weeks. The whole story might have passed by without murmur except that a British Scenic photographer, who happened to be in the area at the time, came upon the scene and contacted the Times of London. Our story became front-page news. The Vandeleur Evictions were discussed in the House of Commons.

It took two long years of great hardship and desperate negotiation before us and the other Vandeleur tenants were back on our land once more. This time we were there to stay, paying and owning the land. Kilrush House, the Vandeleur residence, was destroyed by fire some years later and never rebuilt. Its walled garden is a tourist attraction now.

As you can understand, money was in short supply and with a large family, things were very difficult at home. A chance came for two of us to go to America. My brother Walter and I went to a household in Boston, he to work in the coach-house with the horses and I as a housemaid. We sent home as much money as we could.

Years went by and Walter married. He moved to Atlanta, Georgia, with his new wife and I was bereft without him. But fortune favoured him, thanks be to God, and he opened his own business in the city.

When their first baby was born I went to help a while but that while extended until I became a fixture in the household. They were kindness itself to me but the 'flu epidemic took the lot of them with one fell swoop. There is nobody left of the Atlanta Connells except myself. The Carradotia Connells remained on in Carradotia; they are still there today.

I never went back to Ireland, only in my dreams. Letters tell me that there is a new slated house in front of our old thatched cottage.

Come with me. Come back to Erin, Mavourneen. Let me trace, with trembling finger, the outline of the place where the battering ram did its awful job on that glorious summer's day in July 1888.

LETTERS TO KIMBERLY
BY RICHARD LYSAGHT,
Walkinstown, Dublin

After mother's death, a row is brewing over a large pile of letters written by her over the years to the baby she had given birth to when she was a teenager, and had been forced to give up

'Tricia, mother wanted you to burn those letters, not read them, and certainly not do what you intend doing with them,' Mark, my brother, said from where he stood with his back to the sink. 'And another thing, even if you do find out where Kimberly is, sending her those letters will only cause grief in her life. Is that what you want? It is the last thing our mother would have wanted, I can tell you.' He took a deep breath, shook his head and sighed.

'You're twisting things, Mark.' I said, lifting up a slice of toast and putting it back on my plate without touching it.

'I'm not.' He said, his face reddening.

'You are.'

'Look,' he took another deep breath. 'The bottom line is this: our mother wanted those letters burned.'

'I'm only doing what I believe is right; what I believe ought to be done.'

'Exactly,' he said, his eyes bulging, 'Do you not understand that this has nothing to do with what you believe; it has to do with what our mother wanted. We both heard her. We both were at her bedside, were we not?' He folded his arms in front of his chest, his eyes glaring from a face now fire engine red. 'Well?'

I looked at the thick bundle of letters and the photograph sitting on top of them.

Up to a few weeks ago, I thought this black and white photograph of a day-old-baby, found with the letters my mother wanted burned, was of me or Mark. It wasn't till I read some of the letters that I found out the baby in the photograph was

Kimberly; a baby my mother had when she was a teenager; a baby she had been forced to give up.

The letters were addressed to Kimberly and spoke of my mother's love for her. All ended with the words, 'I love and think of you every day and will do so till the day I have no breath.'

Reading the letters, and there were more than two hundred, I figured my mother must have written them in those times when she was feeling down. I remember seeing her slip quietly up to her bedroom leaving dad, Lord rest him, to keep us entertained.

Once, when I needed to use the bathroom, I saw that her bedroom door was slightly open. I peeked inside. She was sitting on the side of the bed writing. On her bedside locker a candle burned in front of a photograph. I was tempted to go in and ask her who she was writing to but didn't. Now, gazing at the letters, I wished that I had done so; might have saved all this trouble.

I lifted a cup of tea to my lips and blew across the surface to give myself time to think of something to say to Mark. I could think of nothing. Time to garner support from my loving husband, Kevin, who was sitting across the table from me hiding behind a newspaper.

'What do you think, Kevin? Kevin!'

He closed the paper. 'Pardon, didn't hear…'

'I want to know what you think.' I said, putting sugar into my voice; the way I always do when I want something from him. 'Do you think I'm wrong keeping my mother's letters and doing what I feel should be done with them.' I added more sugar and stirred it with a warm smile 'or do you think that Mark is right,' I cringed, 'that the letters should be burned. Give your honest opinion.'

A look of a child caught with his hand in the chocolate biscuit tin just before dinner came over Kevin's face as his eyes darted from me to Mark, back to me, and repeated the process.

'Well?' I said, narrowing my eyes and pressing my lips into an invisible line.

He took a deep breath, grimaced and shifted about on his chair. 'Well, er, since you want my honest opinion, I would have to, er, um, agree with Mark.'

'What?' I said, tempted to ask him who cooked and cleaned for him, was mother of his two golden haired daughters, but I didn't want to sound petty and childish, not in front of Mark, and besides I knew my opportunity to roast my brown-eyed darling traitor of a husband would come later.

'Well, your mother never told you about those letters until ...'

'But she did tell me about them.' I said,

'Yes, but you are misconstruing what she said.'

'I'm what?' I shook my head, biting back the urge to tell him that he should apply to the four courts as a reserve judge.

'She only said that she wanted them burned, never said that she wanted anyone to read or do ...'

'Because she was very ill and didn't know what she was saying, that's why. Besides, she would hardly have a problem with me reading them or deciding what to do with them. I'm her daughter, am I not?' I leaned across the table towards him.

He flinched.

'Well, you could always keep the photograph of Kimberly. No need to burn that. Your mother didn't say anything about the photograph. If it were me, I'd keep the photograph.'

'How thoughtful and considerate of you Kevin,' I said, acid in my voice.

'Of course, it is only my opinion.' he said, and then attempted to excuse his treachery by adding in a voice that held the squeaky fear of a mouse being chased by a hungry cat, 'you did ask me, you know.'

'Thanks, Kevin, I won't forget your honesty, I promise you.' I said, through gritted teeth.

He whipped open the newspaper and disappeared behind it.

'Well there you have it, an independent view.' Mark said, swaggering over to the table, beaming a smile that if it had been any brighter, I would have had to take the sunglasses out of my shoulder bag, hanging from the back of my chair, to stop myself from being blinded.

'I hope you now understand, at last, that you should burn those letters,' he said, and in a condescending tone added, 'keep the photograph of Kimberly, as Kevin suggests.' He squeezed my left shoulder.

I jumped up. 'Oh, I understand alright.' I shook my head. 'I was crazy to think that either one of ye would understand. Ye are men, aren't ye?' I grabbed the bundle of letters, my shoulder bag and stormed out of the kitchen.

'Where are you going?' their voices called in unison.

'I'm going to see Cynthia Byrne, a person whose understanding extends beyond the sized and shape of a ball.' I shouted.

'You're making a big mistake going to see her,' my brother called after me.

I slammed the door shut.

Now sitting in Cynthia Byrne's front room, staring at the yellow crescent pattern on her red carpet, I was thinking Mark was right. The reception I received at Cynthia's front door was one of cold indifference. In fact it wasn't until I said that I would like her advice about a personal matter that the pouchy grey eyes deigned to acknowledge my presence and the stone set lips parted. 'Well, I suppose, you had better come in then, hadn't you.'

This welcome from a woman who had been my mother's best friend since childhood had me clutching my shoulder bag to my chest. Oh, I was aware my mother and Cynthia had a huge falling out, God knows why, several years ago and had only got back talking a week before my mother passed on. In fact, mother had asked for Cynthia, and Mark had collected her and brought her to the hospital.

The sound of cups rattling on a tray sent a quiver of trepidation up through me. No doubt, the same quiver had often been felt by the pupils in St Edna's primary school when Cynthia was still teaching.

She laid the tray on a coffee table. 'Help yourself to sugar and milk,' a bony hand mottled with the blue of age shoved a plate of assorted biscuits in my direction. For the next few minutes I nibbled a chocolate covered biscuit without tasting it. I was too aware of Cynthia who sat in an armchair facing me, her head pressed against a doily the same colour as her white hair, her knurled fingers steepled in front of her chest, her lined face preserving the stoic attitude of a teacher waiting for a pupil to recite the poem given as homework.

There was no way I would talk to this woman. I decided to leave. But before I could think of a suitable excuse to dignify my departure, Cynthia said, 'And what is this matter upon which you wish my advice?'

'Oh, it's nothing really,' I said, my face flushing. 'just me being woman-silly, as my husband and brother say.'

'Bah, men, a stuffed cat has more understanding when it comes to matters pertaining to women.'

I smiled; part of me was getting to like this woman.

'Please, tell me.'

'Well,' I said, putting my cup and saucer down on the coffee table and tightening my fingers round the edges of the bag in my lap, 'it has to do with my mother.'

When I finished telling my story, Cynthia pressed her head harder against the back of the chair. 'Kimberly.' she said with a sigh and let the name float in the air for a few seconds. 'You know, I was the one who took that photograph. My God, your mother was a slip of a thing, then. We both were. Innocent, naïve, hearts as soft as whipped cream.' Cynthia eyes drifted over my left shoulder.

I watched her, watched her pouchy grey eyes glisten with the tears of memory and listened as her lips whispered the past back to life.

When Cynthia did return to the present she jolted me with the sudden staccato tone of her words. 'So, you, young lady wish to know what you should do with those letters.'

I nodded, digging my nails into my bag.

'Did you know, those letters were partly responsible for your mother falling out with me?'

I shook my head.

'Yes,' she sighed. 'When I first came back here to teach, after more than twenty years teaching abroad, I went to see your mother and she showed me those letters. She told me she wrote them in case Kimberly ever came looking for her.'

143

Cynthia's eyes misted and she became silent for a few moments before saying in a croaky voice, 'it broke my heart, not only to see the letters but to think that she was still writing them. I decided then that I would have to tell her what I, myself, had only recently found out.' Cynthia sighed, the most forlorn sigh I had ever heard and muttered, 'never should…'and then her voice trailed off.

I moved to the edge of the chair, my heart in a panic. 'Told her what, Cynthia?'

Cynthia gazed at me for several seconds and then in a strangled voice said, 'that Kimberly was dead.'

'What!' I almost jumped off the chair.

'She had had an undiagnosed congenital heart disease; she died before her second birthday.'

'But how did you …'

'Find out? Cynthia said. 'From a relative I had gone to visit just before I came back here. You see, your mother's parents and mine were very close, and it seems that they decided that Kimberly would be adopted by a wealthy relation of my mother's who lived in Somerset in England. Your mother, when I told her, accused me of always knowing.'

Cynthia sighed again. 'Things were never the same between us after that. I often wished that I hadn't…' Cynthia shook her head, and for the next few minutes descended into her own hell of regret.

I sat watching her, tears rolling from my eyes, tears for the heartache my mother must have felt when she heard that Kimberly had died; the misery she must have endured knowing that Kimberly would never see those letters; letters she could not bring herself to burn. I wiped the tears from my eyes with a tissue, blew my nose and stood up. Cynthia joined me and we both hugged each other for a long time.

'Do you think it would be wrong of me to hold on to some of the letters; just to show my children what sort of a woman she was?' I said, breaking the embrace.

'No, but keep in mind as long as they have you, they have her. You are your mother when she was a slip of a thing.'

'Thank you.' I said, smiling and crying.
'Will you come visit me again?'
'Try and stop me.'
We hugged.
Outside, I rang Mark's mobile and asked him where he thought we should burn our mother's letters to Kimberly.

Memories

LEAN TIMES
BY TOM WINTERS,
Drogheda, Co. Louth

*Times were tough for young Irish emigrants in London in the early
1950's when war-time rationing was still in force*

The only time I was ever hungry in my life was when as
a young man of nineteen years of age I lived in London
in 1952. War time rationing was still on in England and
two ounces of cheese as a special treat for Sunday's tea was the
nearest we got to an appetising meal.

My wages was small and when I paid £2-50 a week for my
digs and sent mother a pound home to help out with her bills I
had very little left for luxuries, maybe the occasional take-away
of fish and chips. We would get a couple of spam sandwiches
that our landlady, Ethel, called a packed lunch to take to work
for our midday- break. Spam was something that mother never
dared give us back in Ireland.

When we returned to our digs at about 7 o' clock in the
evening dinner was always the same, a concoction of grisly meat
and dried-up peas and potatoes that was not very appetising but
always welcome to my ever hungry pals Dermot and Mick, and
myself.

We had little entertainment except a game of cards that we
usually played for halfpennies in our bedroom and a long walk
from the Elephant & Castle on Sunday afternoon to Speaker's
Corner in Hyde Park to listen to wonderful speakers on their
soap boxes.

They talked about every subject under the sun, men like
Donald Soper, Moderator of the Methodist church in England,
and the philosopher Freddie Ayer. There were black men raging
about the treatment of the native peoples of Africa by their
colonist masters, and old soldiers going on about their treatment
when they came home from the war.

I'll always remember one old soldier going on about Lloyd George and his promise of "Homes fit for Heroes" and how he was living in a slum ever since.

We certainly got a free education on the ways of the world and often wondered if listening to the speakers in Hyde Park or having the opportunity of seeing the great City of London with its great buildings like St Paul's, Westminster Abbey and Cathedral and Buckingham Palace was worth going hungry to see.

I'm not talking about famine hunger here, just not filling our bellies like we did at home in Drogheda, with nice fresh eggs, plenty of tea and bread for breakfast, cabbage and bacon and nice warming stews and rice pudding for dinner.

We spent time in the lovely parks like Regent, Hyde and Green Parks; we saw the great shopping areas such as Oxford Street, Regent Street and Bond Street, and we were shocked by the wartime damage around St. Paul's, inflicted by the Luftwaffe.

Our saviour in the London days was the large amount of cheap Victoria plums we eat, and occasional portions of jellied eels, something I had never seen in Drogheda even though we lived only a few miles from the fishing village of Clogherhead.

I often wondered if our deprivation was worth it.

When Mick told us of seeing Ethel's daughter Rose picking up old discarded tomatoes from the ground of our local street market, it nearly put me off eating our grisly meat stew; only nearly, because I was too hungry to complain to our landlady.

It was after a poor Christmas, notable for its lack of turkey and ham, that we decided to return home. Although money was scarce, I was determined to return home in some style, even if I was much thinner, dressed in a nice navy suit I had bought in Burton's Gents Outfitters.

Our chances of getting jobs might be poor, but Mick, Dermot and I set out from Euston Station with five pounds each in savings after our year's hard work and near starvation.

Arriving in Dublin the first thing we did was buy a batch loaf and a block of Galtee cheese, go into a pub, order three pints of Guinness sand have the most memorable feast of our lives up to then.

THE EARLY RISER
BY RAYMOND FENNELLY,
Abbeyfeale, Co. Limerick

*The old people used to say that if you had the name of an early riser
you could stay in bed until dinner time. Mossie Joe didn't have the
name of an early riser and he would have happily stayed in bed until
tea time if he was allowed*

Mossie was an only child and lived with his widowed
mother in a council cottage on the outskirts of town.
The poor woman was worn out from calling him for
school every morning.

"Mossie Joe, are you awake?" she would shout down to him
below in the room

"No Ma. I'm still asleep." the rascal would respond before
turning over and closing his eyes again. He was rarely on time
for school and would usually stroll in after the first break.

"Late again, Mossie Joe" remarked the teacher.

"Better late than never, sir," replied Mossie.

The teacher said that Mossie Joe had brains to burn, but was
much too smart for his own good. "That fellow will go far,"
he predicted. ("And the farther the better." he added under his
breath).

Despite hardly ever opening a book, Mossie left the national
school with a good grasp of reading, writing and "doing the
sums" as he called it. He immediately signed on at the local
labour exchange where he soon became something of a legend.

To prove that he was actively looking for work Mossie
perused the jobs pages of local and national newspapers and
applied for every vacancy that was advertised. These included
the position of Chief Executive of Bord na Mona, a Lecturer in
Joycean Literature at Trinity College, and Head Beer Taster at
the famed Guinness Brewery in Dublin

"What job have you applied for this week?" the counter staff would jokingly inquire.

"NASA was looking for a few men to go to the moon," Mossie answered, handing in yet another letter of rejection "but they turned me down. They said I had no head for heights."

"See you next week." the amused clerk said, stamping his dole form and sending him on his way.

Mossie eventually realized that his career prospects at home were somewhat limited, and he decided to spread his wings. He borrowed money from the mother and set sail for England, ending up in a dilapidated bed-sit above a betting office in the Ladbroke Grove area of North London.

The local job centre was just around the corner and he signed on there each week while he continued his quest of finding suitable if somewhat eccentric employment. He soon learned that the social services in England were not as sympathetic as their counterparts at home, and he was forced, somewhat reluctantly, to accept the position of messenger boy with the John Laing Construction Company.

Each morning he arrived at their head office in Victoria Street and was given his various assignments for the day. These involved visiting the many building sites around London and delivering plans, invoices, pay slips, time sheets, forms etc and collecting orders for any goods and materials that might be required for the following day.

He travelled by tube and, during the journey he would open the different confidential letters and files to find out what was going on. He became well known on the building sites and would laugh and joke with the various brickies, chippies, plasterers, plumbers, dumper-drivers, etc.

They showed him how to mix mortar and lay blocks, how to cut timber and measure door frames, how to lay pipes and install central heating. The architects even spread out their blueprints and explained how the building projects were designed.

Mossie was a quick learner and was soon laying the occasional row of bricks or putting in teak windows and doing other bits and bobs, as well as his normal duties. He rapidly became something of a handy-man in all aspects of the building trade.

He stuffed a few pounds in an envelope and wrote home to his mother telling her that he had secured a responsible and highly-paid position with the biggest building firm in England.

The mother was delighted. "Mossie is getting on great over in London." she told the crowd in the post office when she went to collect her pension. "He is working away every day, so he is, and he have his own place as well."

A couple of months went by and Mossie wrote to the mother again to tell her that he had been promoted to site supervisor.

"Mossie has been made a foreman" she informed the crowd in the post office "and he have men under him now." The crowd was suitably impressed, and news of Mossie's rapid rise in the construction industry was soon the talk of the parish.

"I always said that fellow would go far" the teacher smugly reminded everybody "and I have been proved right."

Six months after going to England, Mossie came home on holidays. He wore a pin-stripe suit that he had purchased in an Oxfam shop in the Tottenham Court Road, and brandished an ivory-handled umbrella found abandoned on the Bakerloo Line between Harlesden and Maida Vale. He borrowed money from the mother (explaining that he hadn't had time yet to change the bit of sterling) and away with him down to the local pub.

He walked into the crowded bar, looking every bit the successful business man, and received a standing ovation. Making his way somewhat sheepishly to the counter, he extracted a roll of borrowed punts from his pocket and quietly ordered a drink for the house. This provoked another sustained bout of raucous cheering and enthusiastic back-slapping.

Mossie retired to a corner table with a glass of orange juice. Former friends and acquaintances gathered to shake his hand and congratulate him on his good fortune. He modestly accepted their plaudits but kept his own counsel. He stayed for an hour and then slipped away into the night.

He was up early the following morning and sat at the kitchen table reading the newspaper while his mother bustled about preparing breakfast.

"Will you be staying at home for long?" she asked.

Mossie folded the newspaper and put it to one side. "I'll be here for a few weeks, Ma" he answered. "The company is expanding into Ireland and I'm hoping to get planning permission for them the build a few houses down below in the village. This is all very confidential at the moment," he added, "and you must tell no one."

"My lips are sealed" promised his mother, already grabbing her coat and hat and half way out the door, all thoughts of breakfast now forgotten.

Mossie smiled and re-filled his tea cup. He sat back and waited for the sparks to fly.

The local bank manager was first out of traps. His big shiny Merc came flying up the boreen and stopped with a squeal of brakes. The front door almost came off its hinges as Mahony bounded in around the kitchen.

"I hear" he said without preamble "that you are planning a housing scheme here in the village."

"Who told you that?" asked Mossie.

"I have my sources" said Mahony, sitting down and opening his brief case. He extracted a sheaf of papers and laid them on the table. "The bank would like to finance the deal" he went on, "subject to the usual terms and conditions of course."

Mossie shook his head. "We have our own finance section," he said. "They look after all the money."

"Why would you give the business to strangers?" asked Mahony. He shuffled through his papers and pulled out an official-looking form.

"I have here," he said "outline planning permission for twenty houses on a prime site just outside the village. The bank has the option to purchase the land for half nothing. We were just waiting for the right developer to come along."

"I don't know." said Mossie doubtfully. "This all seems very irregular and not a good way of doing business."

"Business is business, whatever way 'tis done." answered Mahony diving into his briefcase again and producing a brown envelope and sliding it across the table. "Here is a few bob on account to cement the deal. And there's plenty more where that came from." he added

Mossie slowly opened the envelope and examined the pile of neatly-folded banknotes inside. "You'll be wanting a receipt for this?" he asked.

"Indeed then I won't." replied Mahony. "We'll keep the paperwork to a minimum."

He closed his briefcase and stood up. "I'll secure the title deeds on the land immediately and open a credit account in your name" he said, extending his hand "and here's to a long and profitable partnership."

Mahony drove back down the boreen and nearly collided with a small builder's truck that was just turning in the gate. The truck continued up to the house and Kiely, the local tradesman, strode into the kitchen with a roll of architectural blueprints and drawings tucked under his arm.

"There is a rumour going around that you are about to build a scheme of houses here in the village" he said, getting straight down to business, "and I would like to tender for the job."

Mossie shook his head in apparent frustration. "Is there nothing secret in this place anymore?" he asked.

Kiely spread his drawings out on the kitchen table and embarked on a long and detailed explanation of their contents, but Mossie stopped him in mid flow.

"We will be bringing in our own contractors in from England." he said. "That is the way the company always operates."

"And why would you give the work to strangers when we have some of the finest tradesmen right here in our own village?" Kiely protested. "We have the best of block-layers, carpenters, plumbers, plasterers and labourers. And they will work a lot cheaper than some union crowd from London."

Kiely began to pour over the drawings a second time, but again Mossie stopped him. "Just show me the bottom line." he said.

Kiely pulled out a cigarette packet and did a few swift calculations in pencil on the back of it. "We can build each unit for that" he said, indicating a figure to Mossie, "and the market value should be around that" he added, indicating another figure, far in advance of the original amount.

Mossie took the cigarette packet and checked the numbers. The profit margins were enormous. However, like any good poker player, he hesitated and allowed his opponent sweat for a little bit longer.

Kiely waited anxiously, and then reached into his pocket and produced a brown envelope and slid it slowly across the table. "A little something to show our good faith and perhaps sweeten the deal." he murmured.

Mossie delayed another moment and then decided to put him out of his misery. "I'll have our lawyers draw up a contract immediately." he said, opening the envelope and checking its contents.

"Ah, there is no need for contracts." protested Kiely. "We are all friends here. And sure we don't want to be bringing the tax man down on top of us. What he doesn't know, won't trouble him."

"Very well, so" said Mossie. "You can start whenever you are ready. The bank below is looking after the finances. And I'll hang on to the fag box, just in case." he added.

Kiely took his departure, but he was no sooner gone than Moran, the local auctioneer, pulled in to the yard.

"I'm here about the new houses" he explained, as he opened the door and came into the kitchen.

"This place is getting busier than Piccadilly Circus," observed Mossie, pulling out a chair for the new arrival.

"The news is all over the village" continued Moran, "that you are embarking on a major building project that could add millions of punts to the local economy."

"I wouldn't go that far." said Mossie. "We are just building a few houses. We still have to sell them."

"And that is why I am here" declared Moran. "I'd like to be the sole selling agent for the new development."

"We have our own sales department in London" said Mossie. "They take care of all the advertising and the selling of properties for us."

"Why would you give the business to outsiders" asked Moran,

"when we have an excellent auctioneering business right here in the village?"

"Are you sure that you could handle such a big project?" asked Mossie. "There is a lot at stake here."

"Not a bother!" replied Moran. "In fact I have already had several inquiries from interested buyers. The building business is booming at the moment and there is a desperate demand for new houses."

Mossie said nothing more, and Moran squirmed uncomfortably in his chair. He then reached into his inside pocket and passed a brown envelope across the table.

"Here's a little something in advance," he whispered, almost apologetically "just to show our appreciation."

Mossie took the envelope and gave a cursory look inside. He then stood and shook hands with Moran.

"Welcome to the firm." he said. "Get out there and sell our houses."

Moran left and Mossie decided to go back to bed. It had been a busy morning but, he believed, a profitable one.

Work on the houses commenced almost immediately and within six months the development was completed, on time and under budget.

The local TD gave a speech at the opening and cut the ribbon. The Parish Priest sprinkled holy water and said a few prayers. The new residents received their keys and moved in. Everybody seemed happy.

Moran, the bank manager, called to see Mossie to inform him that another parcel of land had become available.

"He is on the phone to England at the moment." said Mossie's mother, as per instructions. "He said to call back this afternoon."

Below in the room, Mossie awakened briefly before turning over and going back to sleep.

It was true for the old people. When you had the name of an early riser, you could stay in bed until dinner time.

GOLDEN GLOW
BY CLAIRE BUCKLE,
Hornchurch, Essex

*Colm gives the impression of being a bit uncaring and unhelpful
about the big event coming up, but he has his reasons ...*

Colm shrugged off his rucksack, dropping it to the ground
with a thud. It was quite a hike from the house to the
river and these days the effort of walking over the rough
ground often caused him to stop to catch his breath and wipe
the glassy beads of perspiration from his forehead.

Wincing, he loosened the belt of his trousers a notch. He
knew he was carrying too much weight but so what? Hannah's
home cooking had always been his weakness, yet he'd somehow
managed to reach retirement without *too* many visits to the
doctors. He sighed, remembering his wife's pursed lips, as she'd
cut him a wedge of her delicious fruit brack that morning.

"There's a slice of your favourite for your lunch, along with
the sandwiches."

Her mood as she'd packed his bag had signalled disapproval.
Colm, seated at the kitchen table with his early morning tea, had
drained the remains from his mug.

"Well, thank you, love," he'd replied reaching for her hand,
touching her fingers before she shook them away.

"Don't try and get round me Colm Boyle. You're off on one
of your jaunts when we need to get to the supermarket for the
barbecue food - or have you forgotten everyone's coming at the
weekend for our Golden Wedding Anniversary?"

"All right, all right!" he'd soothed. "We'll get the shopping
soon. I just need the fresh air today and the walk to the river
will do me the power of good." He'd patted his generous belly.
"Now let me have that bag so I can pack my fishing gear."

"I might as well get Aoife to take me then," Hannah had
sniffed, pecking him a goodbye kiss, albeit begrudgingly. As the

youngest of their six, even in her thirties Aoife still possessed the outspoken, defiant nature which had made her childhood more of a challenge than all the others put together. Well, why not let Aoife take her, he thought, they could grumble about him to their heart's content.

He looked around, appreciating the intoxicating silence. Only a few miles from town but with not a soul in sight, this was a hidden paradise. Hannah had enjoyed the long walks once but since the arthritis had set in she'd grown reluctant to venture far from the house on foot. Colm's eyes misted, remembering their first kiss, not too far from this very spot. It was over fifty years ago and they'd been strolling along when he'd suddenly stopped and pulled her towards him, placing both hands on her tiny waist.

"Why, Colm Boyle, what *do* you think you're doing?" she'd giggled, as Colm had hesitatingly bent and brushed his lips on hers. Next moment, she'd been circling his neck with her arms and they'd kissed with a passion that looked set to last a lifetime.

A trickle of sweat on his cheek brought him out of his reminiscing. Reaching into his pocket for his handkerchief, he unfolded the exact ironed square and dabbed it over his face. He wiped his nose, threaded with tiny veins, the result of too many 'medicinal' whiskeys, as Hannah would scold him in her sternest schoolmarm voice.

She'd been a strict but fair schoolteacher whose heart could melt as quickly as springtime snow if a pupil brought her flowers, or painted a picture for the classroom wall. Scooping up his rucksack he gave it an affectionate pat before throwing it over his shoulder. He'd not had much time for hobbies in recent years, working long hours to give his large family the life they deserved. He didn't begrudge a moment of it but now was *his* time. Striding out with renewed energy he headed for the mooring.

The sun had burned off the morning mist and was high in a cobalt blue sky by the time Colm, puffing more than he'd have liked, arrived. It looked set to be an unusually hot autumn day and he squinted as he focused on the vibrant trees, noting how the abundance of light reflected their vivid colours in the calm parts of the river. Although the once red paint on the canoe was now pale, crisp and peeling, like a faithful friend Colm knew the boat could be trusted. Anticipation swelled inside him as he untied the rope and climbed into the boat, steadying himself as it rocked gently in protest at his bulk.

"Dad!"

A shout from behind him caused him to turn sharply, almost losing his balance.

"What the..." He was astonished to see Aoife standing on the riverbank, red in the face and breathing heavily. It looked as if she'd been running hard.

"Well, blow me," Colm smiled, "I was just thinking about you." It was a smile not returned by his daughter.

"Just where do you think you're going, Dad?" Aoife blasted him. "Mum wants help with the shopping for the weekend – your 'special day', remember? And you're off on one of your jaunts – unbelievable! Honestly, you could at least pretend to be excited about the weekend for her sake."

Colm slowly shook his head. "Oh, Aoife," he sighed. "So, what's happening- are you taking your mum, or have you just come to have a go at me?"

"I did come over to take Mum shopping but she went all soft, said she'd changed her mind and would wait to go with you. So I decided to find you instead – I knew you'd be off fishing in that old thing."

"Well, you've found me, and since I'm about to leave, how about you calm down and come for a little ride? It's a beautiful day."

"For goodness sake," Aoife exclaimed, "it'll probably sink with both of us on board." Despite her protests, and ignoring Colm's outstretched arm, she clambered into the canoe. "At least this way I'll have your full attention," she added, seeing his amused look.

Colm's large hands lifted the paddle and they started their journey. His broad shoulders swiftly found their rhythm and where the river bubbled and frothed he used his skill to steer the canoe safely through. A mile further down he reached the spot, a quiet sandy inlet shaded by trees.

He paddled the canoe up to the gently sloping bank and he and Aoife got out. As they pulled the boat onto dry ground, Colm looked around, remembering another autumn day, the warm October afternoon he'd first brought Hannah here.

"It's so beautiful, Colm, and so private," she'd said, teasing him with a pretence at shyness.

"I wanted somewhere special where we wouldn't be disturbed. So when I discovered this place on one of my jaunts, as you call them, I decided to bring my best girl here."

Pulling a small velvet box from his pocket he'd opened it and gone down on one knee. Like the river, they'd experienced both rough patches and calm waters, but neither had ever jumped ship and Colm's love for Hannah had never wavered.

Aoife's voice broke across his thoughts. "So why have we stopped here, Dad?" she asked. "You never brought any of us to this place when we were kids."

Retrieving his bag, Colm settled himself on the soft sand and leant against the boat before answering.

"Oh, it's kind of special, love. Private really," he said taking out an old jar, a bottle of water and his recent purchases and setting them on the ground beside him. He gazed across the river, a distant look on his face. "I've been coming here recently to indulge in an old love affair."

A startled frown creased Aoife's forehead and he laughed.

"No, not that kind of affair," he told her fondly. Taking out his sketchbook he flipped it open, revealing the drawing inside. "I used to bring your mum here when we were courting. I'm doing this for her."

The frown disappeared and Aoife's face creased into a smile. "Oh, Dad," she gasped, gazing at the sketch, "it's lovely, Mum's going to be thrilled."

"Do you really think so?" he asked, looking at her doubtfully. "I'm a bit rusty, but…" he raised a hand to point across the river, "the golden glow of the sun through the trees today reminds me of the day I proposed to Mum, right here."

Aoife's eyes were shining. "It's a wonderful idea, she'll love it." She looked sheepishly at her father. "About earlier... I'm sorry for being so angry."

He chuckled. "You've always been feisty so I'm not going to get upset about that," he said, giving her a hug. Then he picked up his brush, ready to mix his watercolours. "Now then, love, all that exercise has given me an appetite. If you look in my bag, you'll find a huge piece of Mum's fruit brack just waiting to be shared."

My First Visit to a Bakery

By Mary Gallagher
Ballisodare, Co. Sligo

A first visit to the big bakery in the town to collect supplies for their country shop still lingers vividly in the memory ...

Heavy cold November rain and sleet slid down the windscreen of the black Prefect. It was a Tuesday afternoon, about sixty years ago. Inside, the aroma of freshly baked bread filled the air and steamed the window panes. This was the next best thing to eating the loaf bread that lay on the back seat of the Prefect.

Soon we would be home and displaying the bread on the long table at the side of the counter in our small country shop. The aroma would linger long into the evening. In the morning the loaves would be firmer, the aroma almost gone or only possible to smell if one lingered long over the bread counter.

I had just accompanied my father to town where he went to replenish supplies for his customers. The first visit as a ten year old still stays in my many memories but particularly in my visual, smelling and tasting ones. Indeed, I have only to pass a bakery or enter one in any town or city to be immediately brought back to my first entrance.

I smile inside as I recall my first meeting with Patsy the Baker. He was a tall strong man with pink cheeks and a warm smile. His shirt sleeves were rolled up high. A long white apron tied around his waist made him look as if he had lived here all his life. His boots were white; he was covered from head to toe with a fine film of white. He stood with a face creamy and pudgy as the dough he worked on at one end of a table.

Bags of yeast sat in the shelves. Large bags of flour were encased in huge wooden presses that opened from the top. He worked, mixing and merging, kneading and unknotting, swelling and reducing, rolling, patting and smoothing the dough until the consistency was just right.

My eyes were wild with wonder as my nostrils wafted in the freshness of newly baked loaves. The intense heat hit me as pleasant on that cold, snowy afternoon. Three long silk-smooth deal tables ran down the length of a large room, two hugging the walls and one in the centre. Row upon row of freshly baked loaves was arranged on the tables, some in baking tins, more on trays. Still more were standing in their cream and brown crispy crust golden dresses.

When he opened the great doors of the ovens I could see into their cavernous depths and conjured up images of the heat of a glowing tomb and wondered if this resembled hell. Periodically he slid a large shovel or spade, with an enormously long handle, into the ovens and retrieved the trays of batch and pan loaves.

He seemed to do his work with ease as he chatted to my father and I continued to grow in wonder at the transformation that was being enacted before me. Then he had a treat for his visitors, or rather for the little girl. He passed me a newly baked hot cross bun that melted on the palate and transported me to heaven for some moments.

I arrived home with a whole new world inside ready to tell my brothers and sister. I had witnessed my mother and grandmother making soda bread but this transaction was of entirely different proportions.

Short Story

THE PRACTICAL JOKER
By Diane Hogarty,
Waterville, Co. Kerry

Funerals are a great excuse for reminiscing and recalling the life and times of the deceased, and some of many antics he was involved in

It wasn't the way I remembered him, to be sure. I was at the funeral of Ger Flaherty, who had passed away peacefully, so I'd been told, in his own bed just a few days ago.

I had to smile to myself as I listened to the eulogy the priest was giving about Ger ... ideal citizen, devoted husband and father, keen member of the Legion of Mary and one of the Sunday readers at Mass.

Don't get me wrong. I'm not saying that he wasn't all of those things, but what I *am* saying is that it certainly wasn't the way I remembered him. Oh no, but then again I'm talking about a very long time ago.

I hadn't been in touch with Ger for donkey's years, must be over fifty to be exact. The last time I'd seen him we were both in our early twenties, and had been buddies for a couple of years. We worked in the same flour mill in Limerick City see, and although we were as different as chalk and cheese, for some strange reason we became great pals.

I've got to admit that I did a fair bit of drinking in those days; well you do when you're young, don't you? Not Ger though, oh no. Ger was a Pioneer and disapproved of the antics I got up to when I'd had a few jars. I don't blame him either in hind sight, because now when I recall the stupid things I did I shudder with embarrassment and fright.

'Your Guardian Angel must work overtime I reckon,' Ger joked one day, and I reckon he had a point there.

Ger never did anything in the least bit dangerous but he was, without a doubt, the biggest practical joker that ever was. And guess who was usually at the receiving end of most of his pranks; yes, you've got it in one, ME!

It's funny, now I come to think of it, that we were buddies at all. I was slim, athletic, and dare I say it myself, pretty good looking. Well, I guess I must have been since so many of the fairer sex took a shine to me.

Ger on the other hand was very over weight, extremely shy where women were concerned and, not to be mean, he was rather ungainly. He wasn't bad looking though and there was a child-like innocence about him.

I'd lost contact with him for so many years because when I was twenty-two I left Ireland and took the ferry to England, thinking I would make my fortune there, or something like that. Of course I didn't, make my fortune I mean, but I did settle down there and it has been my home ever since.

There was a great deal of crying the day I left home and I can remember to this day, even though it was almost sixty years ago, my mother and my five sisters all standing at the front door, wailing their heads off. I was the only boy, see, and I guess in hindsight, spoiled rotten, though I didn't think so at the time.

'Don't forget to go to Mass every Sunday and write once a week will you Pat?' my mother called out as I climbed into my Da's delivery van. He worked for various businesses in Limerick. He was a man of very few words and I knew only too well that he didn't approve of my going to England.

'He'll be back in a few weeks time, you mark my words,' I heard him saying to my mother the previous evening. Whether he was simply trying to cheer her up or whether he actually believed that, I never knew. Maybe he even wished I'd return with my tail between my legs having 'learnt my lesson'; that, too, I'll never know. All I do know is that as I got out of the van he pushed a five pound note into my hand and then he was gone.

That was a very generous thing he did that day; five pounds in those days was a lot of money. He passed away over thirty years ago, God rest his soul, and my darling mother joined him a year later.

The only relations we had in England were my mother's sister Anne and her husband, whom I'd never met. Even though my mother gave me their address in Manchester, I kept telling her that I had no intention of going anywhere near Manchester. London was where I intended to head, where the streets were lined with gold.

Ha ha ... that's a laugh to be sure!

I'm doing my best to remember just how I felt when I finally arrived at Victoria Station after a very long, tiring journey. Scared? Yes, I most probably was. Lonely? Undoubtedly. I was without a doubt what you might call innocent of the ways of the world.

It was all the noise of the traffic that hit me first, then the number of people who all seemed to be dashing everywhere, and lastly the smell of the car fumes. I know it was nothing compared to today, but to me it seemed as though I'd landed in another world.

However, the 'Luck of the Irish' was with me, (either that or all those candles my dear mother was undoubtedly lighting for me!), but within a week of landing in England I'd found myself a reasonable bed and breakfast (two pounds ten shillings a week) and an office job.

I settled in fairly easily, made friends with some fellow immigrants from Ireland, and spent my Saturday nights either at the Irish Club, or going to a dance.

It was at such a dance that six months later I met the girl who was later to become my wife. Mary was from Galway and had come over to England at the age of seventeen to train as a nurse.

Why I'm telling you all this is because I'm trying to explain how it was that I completely lost touch with Ger. The fact was that after I married Mary we very quickly had a family and there was no money over to make trips back home.

On the very rare occasions when I did come over it was usually for a wedding or funeral and consequently there wasn't much time for looking up my old pal.

However, things are completely different now, my family have grown up and have families of their own. So when I was invited to yet another wedding, Mary told me to make a holiday of it and stay for a week or ten days. She doesn't like all the drinking that accompanies weddings, so she said she'd rather stay at home.

Anyway, it was at this wedding that I met someone who knew me before I left Ireland for England, and it was this chap who told me that dear ole Ger had passed away that week and that it was his funeral on the following Sunday.

So... here I am, paying my respects to my dear old pal and tormentor Ger Flaherty, and now I'm going to tell you about one or two of the pranks that old devil played on me.

Ah, I hear you saying, I was wondering when you were going to get down to that! (The wife says I'm always rambling on and if I say I'm going to cut a long story short, it ends up being twice as long, but that's wives for you!)

Out of the countless pranks Ger got up to, two in particular stand out. First though I'd better explain that Ger was brought up by two maiden aunts, why this was he never told me and I never asked. All I know is that these two women doted on Ger. Every day he'd arrive with his lunch box full of neat sandwiches and several homemade cup cakes. Yours truly usually had two thick slices of brown bread with a lump of cheese in the middle, wrapped up in paper.

Being office workers, Ger and I had our lunch in our office, not the canteen, and I usually hid my head behind my paper not wanting to watch Ger demolishing his goodies. Then one day he pulled my paper down and offered me one of his cup cakes.

Of course I should have smelt a rat straight away knowing what a 'foodie' Ger was but I guess I was hungry, so I gratefully accepted it. He handed me a cake with lovely thick custard cream on top which I downed in two mouthfuls then leapt to my feet in horror.

It wasn't custard but mustard on top of the cake, and the hottest mustard at that. I rushed to the sink to fill my mug with cold water and for the rest of the day I must have downed gallons of water while Ger killed himself with laughter. I could have throttled the devil! Needless to say, he never offered me a cake again and if he had I certainly wouldn't have accepted it!

The other prank that comes to mind is this. Ger and I

often spent our weekends cycling round the country and on this particular occasion we were doing the Ring of Kerry and spending the night in a youth hostel. We were tired and somewhat weary by the time we reached the hostel.

'You go ahead Pat and lock up the bikes while I book us in for the night,' Ger told me which I did. There was I thought a very strange atmosphere when I entered the main room of the hostel where several young people were sat on benches.

No one was talking and I thought they all gave me a rather funny look. I must be imagining it, I thought as I sat down on a bench but when a couple of lads moved away from me I knew something was up. Later that evening I asked Ger if he'd noticed anything strange about the reception I'd got when I arrived. At this he burst into a fit of laughter which he could hardly control.

'You did something didn't you Ger?' I said. 'Come on, confess it, I know you've been up to your old tricks. What did you do, you beggar?'

Wiping the tears of laughter from his eyes he confessed that while I was putting the bikes away he'd told everyone that I was a decent enough bloke except for one thing. I was a kleptomaniac, so they'd better beware.

My mouth dropped open in horror, 'YOU WHAT!' I yelled at him, I could have throttled him there and then. I made him go round and explain to everyone that it was a joke, at which they all had a good laugh, including me. Needless to say, I never let him go into a youth hostel again without me beside him.

I haven't told you half of what Ger got up to in the way of pranks, so I suppose you're thinking I wasn't too keen on him. Just the opposite, he was one of the best pals I ever had. If ever I was short of a few bob, which I usually was after a weekend of 'enjoying myself', I could always rely on dear old Ger to tide me over until pay day.

He never ever preached to me either about being more prudent with my money, he wasn't that sort of bloke. Apart from that warped sense of humour he was great, and even then I could usually see the funny side after he'd played one of his 'tricks' on me.

So here I stand, among all the other mourners, saying farewell to a dear friend. As his coffin is lowered into the ground I half expect the lid to open and for Ger's head to appear as he says, 'only joking!' But of course it doesn't. So farewell dear old pal and all I hope is that the angels have as much tolerance of your sense of humour as I had!

THE CARETAKER

By GERALDINE HANNIGAN,
Lifford, Co. Donegal

Warm recollections of a much loved father

'Geraldine, are you up?' The familiar words rang out every morning at ten to eight on the dot. Daddy was always up first. He always made the breakfast. Oooh! How strong he made that tea! I never drank it, but would never fail to complain if it wasn't on the table.

Daddy started work every morning at eight o clock and was rarely late. He was the caretaker in the County Council Offices in Lifford, a very important job, and he was very well respected. He took his job very seriously and would have insisted that I walk to work if I hadn't been ready to go at two minutes to eight.

I worked in the local shirt factory and didn't start work until eight thirty. Some of the winter mornings were so cold, I couldn't bear to walk down the road; I always made sure I got the lift from Daddy. He was a great man, although I didn't realise it at the time, being a cool sixteen year old.

He was a very neat and tidy man. He would shave every morning, no electric razor there. 'I love a good shave,' he frequently declared. I often thought he looked like Santa Claus when he put the soap around his face. He would rub his hands with the soap until it made a fine lather and then he would reach for this funny looking brush he called a 'wabbling brush.'

He used to spread the lather over his chin and cheeks and then he would get his razor and with the precision of a surgeon's hand, he would start the smooth operation. He would gently begin under his nose and using downward strokes he would remove all the lather and I suppose any hair that was there too.

He made very funny faces as he shaved, but when he was finished he would say; 'There now, that's better.' A witty remark would soon follow. He would look in the mirror and say, 'God, you're a fine looking man Eddie, if I was a woman I'd marry you myself.'

On the cold winter mornings he would have the car heater on for me, so that it was nice and cosy for the short journey to work. 'I have you all spoiled,' he would smile as he said goodbye to Mammy who always came down to the nice fire he had lit earlier.

Daddy always loved listening to the news headlines at five to eight before he left for work. That was very important to him. While he loved his work he would frequently complain about how many fires he had to light, which was around thirty.

He had a lot of friends and many would come to the house for a cup of tea. Among those friends was Archie, the sexton in the local Church of Ireland. He would help Daddy with odd jobs in the Council Offices and in turn Daddy would help him with jobs around the Church.

Daddy loved regaling the story to us about the time Archie asked him to dig a grave for a very important man who had passed away. Daddy, being a fine strong man, readily agreed. He toiled hard, digging that grave which was six foot deep and three feet wide, with just the use of a shovel and spade. His sexton friend was very pleased indeed with my father's efforts.

On the morning of the funeral Archie was dressed in his best suit and ready to meet the hearse, and the very important entourage. Daddy strolled around to view the proceedings and, of course, have a little gloat about his perfectly dug grave. Around the corner came the big black funeral carriage, four shining black horses with plumes on their heads and the coach driver wearing his tall hat and black gloves.

He drove very carefully and majestically, the only sound in the quiet street was the clip clopping of the horse's hooves. Six identically dressed men opened the glass doors and began to remove the coffin. There a sharp intake of breath from Archie as a tiny little box emerged; he gasped to Daddy 'Ah Good Lord, Eddie, it's a cremation!'

Daddy fought hard to restrain himself but mirth overcame

him and he almost fell into the grave laughing. Daddy had so many of these stories he used to tell us when we were growing up.

Forty five years later I often dream that I hear those words, 'Are you up Geraldine?'

I wish I was, Daddy, but in the meantime I will listen to the news headlines. I turn off the radio, I wipe away a tear and I answer to the stillness 'Soon Daddy, soon.'

Short Story

THE GREEN SUIT
BY ANNE GALLAGHER
Newry, Co. Down

The old woman has set herself an ambitious task, to create a last, carefully crafted gift in the old traditional way, for her beloved granddaughter

The old woman stands over the ancient Aga stirring the contents of a large, iron pot. She peers, myopically, at the simmering green liquid in the pan's dark depths and her mind goes back to the old granite quarry that held such terror for her when she was a child.

Her mind travels back so often now that the greater part of her life is spent wandering through the world of her childhood and reliving events that remain vivid in her memory, like the fear of falling into that quarry. She sees again the stunted whin bushes that cling to the quarry's sheer walls and, far below, the water.

Even more often than her mother or father, the picture of her granny fills her mind. Her quietly playing with her cousin over at The Rocks, so called because of the great lumps of granite that protruded through the soft, springy turf. Her granny would sit on a mossy bank, her full, black skirts spread out around her.

She could see herself and Nora, her cousin, breaking through head high ferns, their screams and whoops filling het summer air; paddling, barefoot, in the little stream that separated the meadow from the country road, or foraging for hazel nuts or blackberries.

The coals in the fire shift with a soft thud, and the old woman, jerked back to reality, draws the pot stick out of the great preserving pan and peers along its coloured length. The rhythmic stirring has made her drowsy and she goes to the door for a breath of air. The air is crisp and cold for, although the old woman has been up for hours, it is but nine o'clock in the morning.

171

She lifts her faded eyes and gasps at the beauty of the distant mountain blushing in the January sun. She shivers slightly and, pulling her cardigan tight round her, turns back into her cottage. She has work to do, a surprise for her darling Maeve. She loves her granddaughter with an intensity she didn't know could exist.

She opens the press that occupies the alcove between the chimney breast and the wall and takes out a largish parcel, tied with string, which she puts on the table. Her old fingers are gnarled and slow but, with patience, she undoes the knot and spreads the paper wide. Inside are several hanks of wool which the old woman herself has carefully spun.

She remembers, with a chuckle, the look on Packie John's face when, nearly a year before, she accosted him on his way back from tending his sheep on the mountain.

"I want to buy a couple of fleeces off you, Packie John," she said, bold as brass; "when you do the shearing, you know."

"Are you sure it's not a sheepskin you want, missus?" he asked, scratching his head.

"I know what I want," she answered. "I'm not doting yet, you know."

They struck a bargain, there and then, and Packie John delivered the fleeces himself after the spring shearing.

The old woman set about washing and bleaching the fleeces. From the dark recesses of the cupboard and her mind she retrieved her old granny's tools and know-how and painstakingly, she pulled and combed the tangled mess into submission.

She spent weeks in a confused state between past and present. In her more sensible moments she conceded that what she was doing was mad, a goal too difficult to reach. Indeed, the very striving for it was probably accelerating her descent into dotage. Then she would shake herself out of her melancholy and return to the job in hand and her granny's kitchen. She drew the raw wool through the combs and set it, soft and smooth, in a pile ready for spinning. Now, she takes the hanks of wool over to the pan and eases them into the simmering liquid, seeing with satisfaction the pale yarn soak up the colour of the dye.

No shop-bought dye this, not for this labour of love. The

old woman gathered the mosses and lichen herself, just as her granny taught her. An eager pupil, she soaked up the lore like a sponge, as her wool is now soaking up the dye. The colour is just right for Maeve's beautiful, titian hair. The old woman adds the salt which will set the dye and stop it running.

The yarn is ready and the old woman braces herself for this, one of the trickiest parts of the task. Getting the old spinning wheel set up and going again, after years of idleness, taxed her so much that she almost gave up and now she is at another stage which needs her to keep her wits about her.

She is conscious, too, of the passing time. She must be finished and cleared up before her daughter arrives. Her daughter worries about her. The old woman finds her overpowering. She has no soul and would never understand her mother's need to do what she is now doing. So, the old woman keeps it a secret, working during the morning and clearing everything away before her daughter arrives with her lunch, her clean laundry and the newspaper.

Annoyed with herself at the irritation her daughter engenders in her, she tuts and shakes herself before going to the cupboard under the sink and taking out a plastic basin. She will be very careful when she transfers the skeins of wool from the hot liquid into the basin and from there into the sink.

She mustn't scald herself, at all costs, or have any accident. She carries two hanks at a time, across from the Aga and into, what her daughter annoyingly calls the working kitchen, but she herself calls the scullery.

"Bloody stupid" she mutters, giving into a rare moment of blasphemy. She negotiates the seldom used electric cooker. "Working cooker, I ask you!" She's getting tired and irritable and her knees are protesting painfully. At last she is finished and ready to rinse the wool in cold water until the water runs clear.

She looks at the clock, her mind slowly registering the time, half past eleven. She smiles. She can afford the time for a cup of tea. The kettle is never far from the boil, sitting as it does all day on the cooler part of the hot plate.

She carries the big pan, depleted of most of its rich dye, and leaves it on the draining board before wetting the tea. While it brews she busies herself by getting ready a china cup and saucer, milk and a tin of biscuits. She likes this old tin whose lid is a replica penny. An old penny, not one of those stupid wee things that pass for pennies today.

She sits on a hard chair at the table, deliberately avoiding the comfortable armchair. She mustn't fall asleep, not before she has finished her morning's work. It's been a hard, long struggle but she has nearly reached her goal. When the wool is dry she will roll it into balls ready for her final challenge. She has the pattern, the whole magazine indeed, that Maeve had brought some months ago when she had been on a visit. The suit was featured on the front cover and Maeve admired it so.

"Will you keep the pattern for me, Gran?" she asked. "If I leave it at home mum will be sure to throw it out and I want to knit that suit when I finish my degree."

That was what sowed the seed of an idea in the old woman's head. Now only will she knit the suit for Maeve, she will see it through ever step of the way, from the sheep's back to that of her granddaughter.

She gets up and drags her tired body back to the sink to rinse and squeeze, rinse and squeeze, over and over again until the water runs clean and clear as the little brook of her childhood. At last she is done and the pile of wet wool is safe in the plastic basin. The next bit will wait until her daughter has gone so she puts the basin into the cupboard under the sink and goes back to the kitchen and the comfort of her armchair.

Now she can relax and let her mind wander where it will. She shuts her eyes and thinks about Maeve, tall, slender, graceful. How different from the newborn infant, small and frail and so weak they think she will not live; a tiny miracle, born in her daughter's forty third year.

She it was who took over from the frightened mother. She rubbed oil into the paper thin skin of the little scrap of humanity, literally wrapped her in cotton wool and patiently fed the milk into her mouth, drop by precious drop. She lived with them for six months until she had taught her daughter to be a relaxed and competent mother and Maeve a thriving, smiling baby.

She was always on hand to help out with Maeve's upbringing, baby sitting, collecting her from school, taking her to interesting places. There is a special bond between them. Maeve likes to listen to her granny's stories of her own childhood and is always asking her questions. Despite the differences in their ages they are drawn to each other. They are kindred spirits.

She hears the sound of her daughter's voice as from a distance, "It's me mother," and drags herself back to consciousness, only waking fully when she hears the 'ping' of that latest, new fangled contraption that recently appeared in her scullery.

"Do you want it on your knee, mother?" The brisk, down-to-earth voice shatters her mood. She grips the arms of the chair and pulls herself, painfully, to her feet.

"You know I never eat from my knee, Maura," she grumbles. They sit at the table together, her with the portion of dinner her daughter served out for her the evening before when she and her husband had dined. They are both retired now but retain the habits of a lifetime.

"This is very nice, dear," she says to her daughter who is eating a sandwich. "You're very good to me, Maura." She means it too and feels guilty about the negative feelings her daughter brings out in her. "You're so dependable and practical, very like your father, and I appreciate all you do for me. You know that, Maura, don't you?"

"Why shouldn't I look after you, you silly goose, you're my mother!" He daughter gets up to pour them tea and the old woman can't wait for her to go so that she can attend to the wet wool. When it is dry she will be ready to start the most pleasurable part of her surprise.

It is a bright October day and the little graveyard is almost full with the mourners who have accompanied the remains from the small, granite church nearby.

A tall, slender girl, her hair shining like copper in the light of the low sun, stands composed and tearless beside her parents

175

at the graveside. She has cried herself out. She is wearing a green, knitted suit and the people can't take their eyes off her. Oblivious of them all, she is thinking about her grandmother and something Packie John Short said when everyone was swapping anecdotes at the wake.

Absorbed in her own, private grief she just caught the words, "Comes to me out on the road and asks me for a couple of fleeces. Sure, I thought she meant skins, but no, it was the wool she wanted. Amazing, isn't it? I brought them over myself, must have been spring, a year since. Wouldn't tell me what she wanted with them, mind you."

Now the words came back to Maeve and, as the first spade of earth hits the lid of her granny's coffin, the truth about the green suit dawns on Maeve and she cries afresh, her heart breaking.

MACKEREL SUNDAY
By Maeve Edwards
Bray, Co. Wicklow

*The word that the shoals of mackerel have arrived rouses a dozing
Daddy into action and the whole household begins to look forward
to a fishy feast*

A telephone call comes in for my father as he dozes in his chair after Sunday dinner. We shake him awake. "Daddy, Daddy, the mackerel are in! The mackerel are in!"

My father, not known for his speed or his ability to look after himself, rouses himself and begins issuing orders to us children.

"Get my rod, my bait kit, my boots!"

We scatter, gathering up what he needs, wondering why he bothers with anything for each time he returns from a fishing trip like this, he says the same thing. "All we had to do was drop a bucket into the sea and lift a dozen of them out!"

He speeds off up the road in his Vauxhall Viva, leaving us behind with the words: "Get the frying pan ready, mackerel must be eaten as soon as it's caught!"

As if we didn't know!

Our Sunday settles back into its normal dull routine, and we forget all about him for a while. My mother takes out her mixing bowl and before long she has freshly baked brown bread cooling on the windowsill. Its scent warms the air around us and reminds us of the treat we have in store. When she hears the Vauxhall Viva pull up outside the house some hours later, she reaches for a loaf and begins to carve.

Like a caveman returning with the kill, my father enters the kitchen and hands my mother the bucket of mackerel.

"Just for you Alice," he says. We can see the fin tails appearing over the side, and peer in for a glimpse of the shiny blue-green backs, the wavy dark lines, the staring eyes. She takes two carving knives from the drawer and disappears out the back door and down the garden.

We troop after her and watch, fascinated and repulsed all at once, while she beheads the mackerel one by one. Then she takes the sharp knife, guts them and strips out the back spine like a professional fishmonger. The grass in the back garden is like a battlefield, with the seagulls already circling overhead, knowing, by some seagull osmosis, that fish are being gutted in our garden this day.

The cat watches the action from her vantage point on the coal bunker. We throw her a fish head, but she turns away from it, preferring fish in its cooked form. Not for her either the gutted innards which my small brother is now examining with fascinated attention.

The dog is driven demented at the cawing of the seagulls. His taste won't stretch to raw fish either, but nor does he want the seagulls to have it. He patrols the end of the garden daring the seagulls come close. They ignore him, swooping in, with loud screeches and a flash of white wings.

My father meanwhile is busy wrapping mackerel in newspaper and running us sisters up and down the road to the neighbours. As usual he has caught too many but, no matter, a home will be found for it.

"Do you want a couple of mackerel just out of the sea?" we cry while thankful hands reach out for the parcels.

"Thanks, we'll have them for our tea!"

Our mackerel are now floured and lined up on a plate while my mother melts the Cookeen on the frying pan. When the fat begins to smoke, she lifts the first fish by its tail and lays it flesh side down on the frying pan. The pan sizzles and crackles and the delicious scent of frying mackerel fills the air. A quick flip over, the blue black skin shrinking as it hits the hot fat, and fish number one is done.

It's slid onto a plate, and handed to the first child in line. Fish number two takes its place on the pan. Slice after slice of buttered brown bread disappear as each fish gets fried and handed to the next in line. Finally, the last fish is ready and my mother joins us at the table.

"You just can't beat it," she says. "A meal fit for a king!"
"Or a queen actually, Alice," we might have said.

SNOWDROP
BY MUIREANN MACGAFRAIDH,
Athboy, Co. Meath.

Times are tough in Dublin in the early 1900's, with many families trying to survive in crowded tenements; it was not a great place for a sickly baby to begin life, but people rallied round and fought the good fight in face of all adversity

Julia Fitzsimons was a dockers's daughter, born and reared in Rutland Street, just off Summer Hill in the city of "Anna Livia" She was proud of being a Dubliner. Julia was a product of her times, tough times, hard times, fighting times, hungry times. She was born at the turn of the century; the 20th century that is.

She had lived with her parents, two brothers, her older sister Mary and their cat "Ginger" in the two front rooms of a tenement house.

"Ye could eat off the floor in that house it was so clean; ye could! We all took turns to sweep the halls and steps and staircases we did."

Julia pulled her cardigan tighter across her ample bosom. She enjoyed a sing-song with good songs like Kevin Barry or James Connolly and to get it all going she would give a lively rendition of Get Out Ye Black 'n' Tans which she usually sang as she scrubbed the floor. She bashed and beat that scrubbing brush to such a tempo that she needed a strong pot of tea afterwards; a four spoonful job.

Tonight was not a time for singing. Julia was quiet as she pulled the curtains closed. It was a lethal February night. The rain lashed needles and sleet stung cheeks and bare hands. Daybreak had hardly begun with its treacherous winds before it was time to switch on the lights again. She picked up the brown paper bag, blessed herself from the holy water font and stepped out into the night.

The streetlights deepened shadows on old brick walls, road and footpaths. The hall door next door was ajar. The hallway was solid dark but a dim light flickered further down the way. Julia stepped in and called softly "It's only me, Maura." Her sandaled feet padded down the hall and three wooden, rickety steps. She tapped gently and opened the chipped green-painted door into a small room.

A fire burned in the hearth, the opened door caused a downdraught and she got the smoky sweet scent of burning turf. A younger woman was bent over a makeshift cot that in its other life was a drawer; the flames cast her as a giant shadow against the faded floral wallpaper.

"Hello Julia, thanks for dropping in."

"Not at all. How is he?"

"The doctor has been here, he gave him an injection. He said what it was but I can't remember." Her voice shook, her weary hand pushed back an unruly wave of hair.

"Sit down darlin'.. you're worn out." Julia put her arm around the younger woman and guided her to a chair. She was a striking young woman, her blue eyes in contrast to the auburn hair; her face was strained with worry and weariness. Julia's strong warm hands enveloped Maura's ice cold ones as though willing the heat into the cold limbs. Her concerned freckled face gazed deeply into Maura's. "God is good…"

"So they say…"

"He is." added Julia with firm conviction.

Maura lowered her head and tried to hold back the tears. "I know…he's just so little…." she whispered and nodded in the direction of the drawer. She drew a knuckled fist across her lips to force back the sobs.

"I'll make us a pot of tea." Julia pulled a quarter pound packet of tea and a fruit soda from the paper bag she had brought. She headed for the kitchen.

There was a table, some assorted chairs, a gas cooker; a grey metal washing tub and scrubbing board sat on a wooden water stained stand. Newspaper filled the gaps and holes in the floorboards. The walls were papyrus yellow that long ago were white, bilious green paint covered the presses.

Julia filled the kettle from a battered brass tap over an old chipped white Belfast sink and put the kettle on to boil. She found the bread knife cut the fruit soda into slices and wondered how much rent they paid for this dreadful damp place. The hiss of gas, metal and water settled down to a comfortable rattle.

Maura gazed at the tuft of black hair that stuck out of the blue knitted coverlet. The young mother's thoughts gathered momentum and clattered inside her head. He was so little, so sick …Twelve weeks old and going down hill fast. He had come too soon; she had almost lost him but he had fought his way back. The blue eyes looked down at the tiny face, the perfect hands and the parted lips.

Fearful he might die in his first weeks, Julia had fetched the priest and he had been baptized, not in the joyful bright tones of a family occasion, but in the sombre tones of gravitas and urgency Daniel Michael O'Flynn was named. His mother, terrified of the winter weather, had not brought him out of the house. Now pneumonia was his battle and hers.

"Keep him warm, close to the fire Mrs. O'Flynn." The doctor knew well that this was the only heat in the house. "The crisis will come in a few hours. I'll be back." He pulled the door gently shut and left.

"Come on my lad," whispered Maura. "Come on my little manyeen…show your Mammy.." Maura bent and kissed his cheek. The baby stirred as tiny fingers touched hers. Maura heard the clink of spoons on saucers, wiped her eyes and sat back down.

"Here we are," stated Julia, her ginger hair bounced as she came into the room. She moved deftly as she weaved her way like a ship in full sail and placed the wooden tray on a chair.

"Nice and strong; no virgin's water here, as me father used to say."

She placed a cup and saucer in Maura's hands. "Get the heat into yourself now pet".

Maura murmured her thanks. Julia pushed the plate of neatly buttered fruit soda towards her. "Made it this morning."

They sipped hot tea and bit into the buttery sweet flavour of soda cake and were silent, savouring the calmness and friendship of that particular moment.

"It's good of you to sit with us Julia. Michael wanted to sit up but I wouldn't let him. He's bone weary and has an early start tomorrow. He's to collect some boxes off the boat and deliver them to Kilkenny."

"Kilkenny! That's a long old drive. The weather is to worsen, rain is forecast. I listen to the shipping and long range forecast of an evening; I find it soothing…very soothing indeed. Malin Head, Mizen Head, Carnsore Point, great names and said with such surety in cultured tones. It makes me proud to know that the rest of the world might be listening into an Irish broadcast and for them to realise that we are an educated people," she stated and set her empty cup into it's saucer. "Cultured" she repeated with a nod .

Both women grew quiet as the wind howled and banged about the chimney. The gale whistled through drenched darkness and a cat called it's misery in the echo of an alley. Maura's eyes closed briefly and she yawned.

"Now you get a bit of rest. I'll wake you if anything changes." said Julia.

"No, no…I couldn't." replied Maura.

" Just rest your eyes for a little while. Here sit over here at the fire by young Danny.."

"His name is Daniel, Julia; Daniel." retorted Maura.

Julia smiled. "Of course it is pet and a fine name it is too. A brave name, a fighter's name. 'Daniel in the Lion's Den' is in the old Testament. He was afraid of no-one, not Caesar, not the lion, not nobody!" Julia took a crocheted blanket from the back of the chair and tucked it around Maura .

"Now rest your eyes darlin'… "

As Maura slept. Julia kept vigil, turned the radio on low and listened to the melodic tunes and checked on the baby. The rain lashed and the wind rattled the window frame and she remembered another night like this long ago when her Edmund had died. He was her first child, a beautiful boy with the same colour hair as herself and eyes as big and as bright as shining stars.

He was never strong from the start but he had improved and rallied a little. She would cuddle him and laugh as he giggled when she tickled him or washed him in the sink. He was hers and no one would be allowed to hurt him. But he got influenza and there was no turning back.

Her own mother was still alive then. She too was a formidable woman, but he had left them. Left them bereft and full of grief. A desolate sadness that would never leave. Julia had held him as the little body grew quieter and Julia watched her mother take a feather out of her best hat and lean over him and gently pass the feather across baby Edmund's cheeks. The light, gentle touch made the baby smile as he took his last breath, his gentle lips slightly parted, he smiled towards the stars and his mother before his grey eyes closed.

Outside a dog howled and so did the wind on every rattley window and loose hinged door on the street. A movement brought Julia back to the present. She pushed her beads into her apron pocket took out her handkerchief, coughed into it and dabbed it against her lips.

"Germs are terrible things, they get everywhere. Ye have to be so careful."

"What time is it?" asked Maura. "Three o'clock." answered Julia looking at the mantle clock.

"You should have woken me up."

"What for, didn't ye need it? You can make yourself useful by making the tea."

"How is Daniel?" asked Maura as she went over to him. He was uneasy and fractious, his plaintive cry weak and reedy. "The doctor said to give him cooled boiled water during the night." She felt his forehead, her heart plummeted; "Julia, he's so hot."

Julia felt Daniel's forehead. "He's too hot. Get a face flannel or cloth and wet it with cold water. We have to get his temperature down."

Maura raced to a small press by the chimney breast and pulled out two face cloths and ran into the kitchen. She returned quickly, both cloths swimming in a small enamel white and blue rimmed bowl. Julia took the bowl from her.

"You lift him out of the cot darlin'. Hold him in your arms."

"Oh Julia...."

"Pick up yur son Maura, there's a good girl,." said Julia quietly.

Maura held him. Julia sat her down, took a flannel and placed it across the baby's forehead and gave Maura the other to dab on his cheeks. Two hearts pounded silently in unified pitch. The crisis had come but neither said it, afraid to give voice to the words and their implication.

Upstairs the floorboards creaked and Michael coughed in his sleep. It was a rattling cough. As Maura held Daniel she listened to the coughing upstairs. Michael was not a strong man and she knew it. He had caught tuberculosis when he was in the army during the 'Emergency'. The army had treated him but it left him weak. He returned to his job as a truck driver but he was not in good health when he came home.

"These are the dangerous hours Julia. The hours between the darkest of the night and the dawn. "Many go in these hours but not Dann ...Daniel, not our Pluirin Sneachta."

"What does it mean Julia?"

"It means snowdrop in Irish!"

"Snowdrop?"

"Have ye never noticed the snowdrop? It's a delicate little thing of a flower. To look at it you couldn't imagine that such a weak little flower was such a fighter. In the worst of the weather it stirs itself awake. In the depths of snow, in the face of gales, against the forces of nature, it sticks it's beautiful head up through the snow when the rest of nature is in a coma and has no intention of sticking it's head up anywhere.

"There it is, it's face glowing out like a lamp to lighten an' brighten our days, to give hope that the worst is over and Spring is near. Daniel is our snowdrop; a fighter." said Julia with a determined smile.

Maura quietly wept. The baby began to cry. "Don't cry darlin'." whispered Maura . A splash of a tear dropped onto the baby's hand and for a moment the cry was quenched. His mother felt his face. "He's too hot, Julia. What are we going to do? Do you think the doctor will come soon?"

"I don't know but we can't wait on that eventuality, we have to act now. Strip him but leave the nappy on. I'll get another bowl."

Maura's shaking hands unwrapped the blankets around Daniel, her fingers fumbled with tiny buttons. She heard the rattle of enamel bowls and water running, then Julia arrived. "Rub him down all over we'll keep at it till that temperature goes down."

Maura took the face cloth and began to wipe the baby's face and arms and on the other side Julia was rubbing his legs and back. They kept it up for what seemed to Maura like a very long time. She didn't notice how wet or cold she had become. Her arms ached. Daniel had twisted and turned and cried. There came a soft footfall, the door opened, revealing the doctor's tired face. " How is he doing?"

"I don't know doctor. I don't think he's as hot as earlier…it's hard to say. My hands are cold from the water." replied Maura. Julia grabbed a towel and handed it to her.

The doctor leaned over Daniel and lifted him into the makeshift cot and took his temperature. He placed his fingers on the baby's neck. He turned to the women with a satisfied look on his face. "Looks like you won this battle. ladies."

There was a deafening silence until Julia uttered, "God is good." Maura sobbed.

"Tea" said Julia. The doctor reached into his bag and pulled out a small Baby Power bottle of whiskey. "Throw a drop of that into it Mrs. Fitz Simons."

"Whiskey, doctor?!"

"Medicinal purposes only…it'll put the heat into Mammy."

"Of course doctor; a true Christian gentleman you are, so ye are.."

They drank tea. It was hot, strong and sweet. A comfortable silence filled the room. Daniel slept softly.

Suddenly there came the song of a bird as though to affirm that he also had made it into the clear, clean, bright light of dawn; for now, they too knew that their battle also had been won.

Up For The Match
By Aidan Kielthy,
Ballymackessy, Co. Wexford

The ritual of trekking to Croke Park for the big games has been a feature of Wexford and Irish life for a long time. The outcome was often disappointing but this piece recalls a victorious Wexford occasion

The sun had scarcely peeped over the gable end of the old shed, drawing back the shadow as she lifted, than we were on the lawn, hurls in hand. I was Wexford, my two brothers were Kilkenny; they didn't stand a chance; I had Tony Doran on my team.

Tony was a hero in our house, and in most of the houses throughout County Wexford. He had been leading the Wexford hurling attack for many years, enduring lots of hardship as he leaped high to grab the ball on the edge of the square and scoring many swashbuckling goals.

Our mother was inside preparing the sandwiches for the journey, occasionally breaking away to roar instructions not to get our Sunday clothes dirty. As the eldest I also took on the role of the commentator and you could hear the thrill in the voice as 'Michael O'Hehir' lauded the flame haired Doran as he rattled the Kilkenny net for his and Wexford's fifth goal of the day. "The three in a row was dead at the hands of the Buffers Alley farmer!"

My father arrived home from first mass and signalled the end of the epic match with a gesture that left us in no doubt that it was time load into the car, after first ensuring there would be no toilet stops en route.

We met with my aunt and uncle at the local church car park, divided the passenger load and soon the two-car convoy was heading north through Enniscorthy, Ferns and Gorey, on through the Wicklow wilderness towards the Capital for the

1984 Leinster hurling championship semi-final at Croke Park between those age-old rivals, Wexford and Kilkenny.

The roads of 1984 were not what they are today and by the time of the first stop, at the Glen of the Downs, tummies were beginning to rumble. Sandwiches never tasted as good as they did in the Glen of the Downs and the anticipation of what my aunt would provide for a treat afterwards added to the flavour. It was rhubarb tart this day, which was devoured with appreciation.

The cars were parked in a residential area near the stadium and the entrepreneurial attendant was paid his fee, half now and half when we got back and found the vehicles safe and secure.

We were always early for matches in Croke Park. My father liked to 'soak up the atmosphere' as he put it. My brothers were both lifted over the turnstile but to my immense sense of importance, I got to walk through.

Normally such a mild mannered calm person, something seemed to happen to my father, who we sadly lost a few months ago, every time he entered a GAA pitch. He became extremely tense and was often quite vocal in his criticism of opponent, referee and sometimes even our own players, but never Tony.

We sat at the back of the old Hogan Stand where, even on a pleasant June afternoon, the wind could sweep in and almost cut you in half.

For the most part the memories of the match have faded, but not the last few minutes. Tony Doran grabbed the ball from his full forward position and set to the task of taking on his marker, the bearded and to my ten year old self, fearsome looking, Dick O'Hara. Doran won the battle and palmed the ball to the back of the great Noel Skehan's net to raise a green flag. Wexford had beaten the reigning All Ireland champions in the dying seconds.

The elation was overwhelming and for the first time in my life I witnessed grown men cry. Interestingly, that day a member of the fantastic Fitzhenry dynasty, Martin, made his senior championship debut in the purple and gold, and if memory serves scored 2-3 from play. However, as he had done countless times before, Tony stole the headlines.

The journey home from Croke Park is often long and slow as tiredness replaces the excitement and anticipation of the trip up, but not this day. We could have walked home, if required, without complaint. Every beep of the horn from a Wexford car was reciprocated on the double by my father and cheered loudly by his passengers.

When we stopped in Ferns that evening for the customary bag of chips, the streets were filled with like-minded hungry supporters, each as buoyant and delighted as the next.

We arrived home that night some twelve hours after we left. My efforts to return to the lawn were thwarted by my mother who directed me towards my bed. My father said nothing and I got the impression that, had he been let, he would have joined me that night for a game.

Tony Doran only played one further time for Wexford, the defeat to Offaly in the Leinster final two weeks later. But half a decade later he returned to Croke Park to complete his medal collection with that most unique of Wexford achievements, a Club All Ireland accolade.

He did, however, play on successfully for many more years in the make-believe games on our front lawn.

DANCING IN THE RAIN
BY DERMOT LANE,
Tyrrellstown, Dublin

The twin sisters were inseparable, doing everything together. There was that memorable summer of shared adventure when the family had a mobile home by the lake, and the silver bracelets they got for their 12th birthdays. Then, tragedy came to visit …

L ife, someone once said, is not about waiting for the storm to pass, it's about learning to dance in the rain.

I was born on a stormy New Year's Day, and my sister Gina followed five minutes later. They tell me I fretted and sobbed, stopping only when they placed her in the crib beside me. That's the way it was with us always, neither ever felt complete without the other close by.

We slept in the same bed until we were nine or ten, often singing ourselves to sleep or making up bedtime stories for each other. I can still remember the comforting sensation of her breath on the back of my neck, as we slept with arms and legs entwined.

One year during the school holidays, our parents managed to acquire a mobile home by the lake. We were to have it for the whole summer. It wasn't far from the city, but was far enough away to feel like a different world to us. Dad had to work but he came down to stay at weekends.

Gina and I spent almost every minute outdoors. We filled our days paddling in the lake, skimming stones, calling out across the water to hear our voices echo eerily back from the cliffs on the distant shore. Occasionally, as a special treat, Dad would bring us to the nearby hotel for dinner. How happy we were then, two tomboys with a long summer of freedom and adventure stretching out ahead of us.

Aunty Joyce sometimes came to stay for a few days. Dad

called her Aunty Joy and she lived up to this name in almost everything she did. She was our Godmother and favourite aunt and loved to buy us presents. For our twelfth birthday she gave us each a silver identity bracelet with our names engraved, so she could tell us apart, she said, laughing. When we put them on we swore a childish oath never take them off again as long as we lived.

One glorious summer morning we begged Mum to bring us for a picnic to the woods at the far end of the lake. It was the last week of our holidays and Dad had already gone back to work. Auntie Joy was there, as eager for the hike as Gina and me, and eventually Mum agreed. As we made our way along the trail, the mobile home became no more than a speck in the distance.

We had never come this far before and it was a great adventure, exploring this new territory. Running on ahead of Mum and Auntie Joy, we hid behind the huge boulders and splashed our way across the little streams that here and there trickled across our path. When we came to the small beach at the head of the lake, we settled there for our picnic.

After lunch, as the day grew hotter, Mum and Aunty Joy set out their blankets and lay in the sun. Gina and I flew around the place, exploring here, collecting coloured pebbles there, running up and back to the woods gathering pine cones and keeping an eye out for the deer and rabbits that Dad had told us lived in the woods.

The heat got to us too and we sat down to examine our collected treasures. We soon became restless again and, bored with that game, decided to go for a paddle in the lake. We changed into our bathing suits and Gina led the way, with me following not more than two yards behind.

To this day I do not know how I lost her. One second she was knee deep in the water squealing at the coldness of it and the next she was gone. I thought she was playing a trick on me and I called her name, telling her not to be so mean. I called her again and again, louder each time. Mum and Joy came running, screaming, frantically searching the water, but she was gone from our sight. Not even a ripple disturbed the surface to suggest where she might be.

And then I felt it. I felt her gasping for breath and instead, breathing in water. I felt her pain as she fell weightless and helpless, the current sucking her under and tossing her about like a piece of flotsam. I felt the pull on my spirit as she died, oh my God how I felt it, an icy grip reaching into the very core of my being and wrenching it in two. I howled a deep, primeval howl, and screamed her name one last time, to be answered only by the lonely echo of my own voice.

We all died a little that day, and every day after that we died a little more as the lake refused to give her up. Eventually, three weeks later, we held her funeral mass and the priest sprinkled holy water over the lake, the final resting place of my other half, my sister Gina.

Eighteen years passed before I could go back to the lake, a thirty year old woman with a broken life. The years of torment and constant nightmares, of trying to fill the hollow void in my life, had worn me down. I needed peace, I needed closure.

The hotel was much as I remembered it; I doubt it had even been painted in the intervening years. The room was small with a well-worn carpet and a patina of nicotine stains on the ceiling. A once white net curtain sagged across the window, through which I knew lay a spectacular view of the lake. It was too dark to see it but I could feel its brooding presence oozing from the blackness beyond.

I rose early the next morning, just before sunrise. There were few people about; everybody was sleeping off the New Year's Eve excesses of the night before. The day had dawned bright without a cloud in the sky, except for the pink flecked vapour trails left by passing planes. A fine mist hung on the shoulders of the mountain, rolling down to settle unmoving across the surface of the lake. A breeze rippled through the rushes where a single heron kept a lonely vigil. I put on my backpack and began the fateful trek that our little group had made all those years ago.

When I reached the tiny beach where we had played on that

day, the memories came flooding back. I didn't block them as I usually did. I wallowed in them, invited them in as welcome guests. I gathered stones like we had done then, this one a ruby, that one a diamond and there, look, a big shiny one. It must be gold! I wrote our names in the sand, ran up and back to the woods and clambered onto the biggest boulder calling her name at the top of my voice, not once but several times and each time the echo called it back to me ... Gina, Gina. Gina.

I gathered up more pebbles and bigger stones and filled them into my back pack until it was full and almost too heavy to lift. I managed to get it onto my back and tightened the belt around my waist, walked down the beach into the water and kept going. I knew I didn't have to walk far before the shallows gave way suddenly into the treacherous depths. Determined, I pushed on and on until at last, the floor gave way and I began to sink.

Soon, those familiar feelings overwhelmed me again, the ones that have woken me screaming every night for the past eighteen years; the gasping for breath, the weightlessness, the agony of separation, but also a new feeling, one not in my memory from that day, a feeling of peace. The last thing I remember before I blacked out was a vague sensation that I was not alone.

I woke up on the shore soaked to the skin and freezing cold. Dragging myself onto my knees and coughing up water all the while, I wondered how I was still alive. It was still early and there was not another person to be seen. I realised my backpack was gone and realised, too, that I was holding something tightly in my right hand.

I unfurled my fingers and held it up to have a closer look. It was a silver identity bracelet, tarnished, but the name was still readable: Gina. I sat for a long time, staring out over the lake trying to make sense of what had just happened. I still can't. But one thing I do know, that sense of peace I felt under the water has never left me. Somehow, and for some reason, I feel whole again.

I put Gina's bracelet on my wrist beside my own and walked back to the hotel. Maybe after all, life is about dancing in the rain.

WHITE HORSES
BY ALAN C. WILLIAMS,
Langast, France

Sheenagh is relaxing at one of her favourite riverside haunts when she has a chance meeting with a famous footballer but their conversation is interrupted when a little boy gets into serious difficulties ...

Sheenagh sat back against the willow tree. It was the only shade on the grassed slope overlooking the estuary and even here, the sun's heat was uncomfortable. Gazing at the waves she scribbled a phrase into her note book.

"Neptune's children?" she thought before dismissing the image almost as quickly as she had considered it. "No, far too sickening!" She erased the phrase from the page before placing the pencil on her lips.

Sheenagh scanned the river beach in front of her. It felt relaxing. Overhead the sun was still hot although the late afternoon sea breeze made it more bearable. There were a number of people basking on the sands and rocks, many already burnt, not yet realising that fact. Elsewhere, families played their simple, fun games, barely aware of the woman beneath the solitary tree. Her gaze returned to the wind tossed waves.

"Rows of snow-capped hills ..." She dismissed that thought as well.

"They're called 'white horses'."

Sheenagh turned her face upward to the male figure standing to her side. He was also looking at the river.

"Excuse me?" she said, conscious that she was seated in the shade and that he was standing. This made her feel slightly uneasy.

"The waves; my mam called them 'white horses', galloping over the water, chasing each other."

Sheenagh turned to the river again, nodding in agreement. "I can see why. Thanks. I've been trying to write something about them in my mind. I ... I write a bit of poetry when I can."

"Mind if I join you?" He gestured, indicating the surrounding area. "It's the only shade on the beach."

"It's all right. I'm going now."

"No! What I mean to say is ... don't go because of me. I'd ... I'd like some company."

Sheenagh examined him through her sunglasses. He was dressed smartly in a crisp, beige shirt with slacks. Unlike herself, hiding behind the glasses, she could see his eyes clearly. He was young, about her age. Although the shirt was a loose fit, she could discern that he was well built ... an athlete, perhaps? She made her decision.

"Okay."

He sat near her although not so close as to make her uncomfortable. They remained quietly, content with their private thoughts whilst staring at the sunlit tableau before them. Upon the sands, a small boy was trying to kick a football. To his left were a number of rocks, wet from the crashing water. Yachts drifted in the distance.

Sheenagh slowly turned her head towards the man. He was sitting on the grass with his arms clasped loosely around his knees. She recognised him now – he was an athlete and a famous one at that.

Before she could speak, he commented on the weather. It was a mundane statement. Sheenagh felt disappointed. She had hoped for some deeper insight. He spoke again, as if reading her thoughts.

"My mother used to bring me here. We'd both lie here watching the waves then imagine we'd be riding them to far off places. China was a favourite for some reason." He paused for a moment and the wistful expression faded. "She died when I was seven. After that ... well, life was never fun again."

"You seem to have turned out all right."

"Yeah. My father took over, said he'd make a man of me."

"And ...?"

"He did!" Sheenagh expected him to continue but he did not.

She noted the angry undertone in his voice as he'd mentioned his father.

"By the way, name's Ronan."

"I know, seen you in the papers."

The child with the ball was still playing. More often than not his efforts left him missing, and then falling onto the sand. Both Sheenagh and Ronan watched, drawn to the shrill screams of delight as the boy raced around.

"Guess you want my autograph?"

"No, thanks." Ronan seemed surprised, so she continued. "Don't bother collecting them."

"Fair enough!"

Sheenagh glanced over to him. He was examining his hands, obviously embarrassed from her rejection. Ronan Stirman, or 'Starman' as the crowds called him. "Football Superstar" or simply a guy with the same problems and doubts as she had? She usually avoided people when she was out by herself, preferring to hide in the shadows. Whatever the reason that she had stayed to chat with this 'celebrity', she had her own problems to resolve and listening to him wasn't helping her.

"You said you write poetry?"

"I'm a teacher. Poetry is only a hobby though I've had a collection published last month. Only a small one but it's something I'm proud of."

"That's great! I love poetry also. All sorts, Keats, Longfellow, Dylan Thomas ... "

Sheenagh eyed him quizzically.

"Yeah, me, a footballer who likes poems! Weird, eh? Get a lot of stick from the rest of the team, but I do enjoy reading them. Favourite's Robert Frost. My father made me give it up at school yet I still love it. Helps me relax and focus."

Sheenagh knew that she had the type of personality that people felt comfortable with. She was a good listener and it helped a lot of anxious people to have a receptive audience.

"I do all right at football but sometimes I wonder ..."

Sheenagh waited, considering if she should prompt him. She decided against it. Instead she peered at the shadow edge in front of her. The setting sun was pushing the tree shade further up the slope, almost touching their feet. She'd have to move soon.

Suddenly, Ronan continued, his voice now even more pensive. "I know you probably don't understand. Frost said it all in one of his most famous poems. Regrets about life's decisions in '*The Road Not Taken*' ... That's me, alright. I feel my whole life is football. My dad made me practice, practice, practice ... all the time, first at school, then the Club."

He scuffed the grass with his heel, watching it as though he expected some deep revelation. "Now I wonder if that's all that I am."

They were both startled when a ball bounced in front of them before rolling to a stop nearby. The boy was running toward them. Ronan stood and carefully threw the ball back to him. The child scooped it up eagerly.

"Thank you, mister," he called out.

Sheenagh began to gather her few possessions - her bag and shoes.

"I've got to go," she said, adjusting the huge sunglasses she usually wore when out by herself. She knew that other people were uncomfortable when they couldn't see her eyes, yet that was never her intention. The glasses simply gave her a sense of privacy, concealing her striking beauty from unwanted attention and comments. A paper bag may have been more effective to hide beneath but it certainly would be much more conspicuous than the sunglasses.

Sheenagh took a last glance at 'her' beach. She lived nearby and often came here. Something wasn't right with the scene.

"Ronan! Where's that small boy gone?"

The young footballer stood up. "Not sure ... With his mam?" he suggested, scanning the beach intently.

"No, she's over there. She's searching for him also," Sheenagh commented, pointing. She was beginning to be concerned.

Suddenly Sheenagh saw the limp form on the rocks.

"Over there!" she called out, pointing.

Ronan's reflexes and speed surprised her as they both dashed to the child. By now, others were coming, including the boy's mother.

He assumed control. The toddler seemed to have fallen over some rocks. His face was under the water in a pool.

"He's not breathing," Ronan announced frantically. He eyed the onlookers, searching for some person who would step forward and announce that he or she was a doctor. Ronan frantically asked. No one moved.

"CPR!" he yelled to Sheenagh. She nodded, moving slowly at first. The footballer told a woman holding her mobile to get an ambulance. In the midst of the gathering small crowd, Ronan took a deep breath, concentrating on the task ahead.

"You do his heart. Not too hard, he's only little," were his instructions to Sheenagh as she knelt over the boy. For the next few minutes both of them worked together on saving his life. His airways were clear but, as each second passed, their despair deepened. He wasn't responding. They could hear the child's mother crying; however she stayed back, aware enough of the situation to allow these strangers to do their job. They were his only hope.

Finally the toddler gasped and spewed water from his tiny mouth. He took deep gulps of air before he tried to move.

"Mammy," he sputtered as she cradled him. He seemed to be all right.

Ronan and Sheenagh stood, to the cheers of the crowd. Although Shannon had removed her glasses earlier in the rescue, it was only now that Ronan noticed her eyes. They were an intense blue. They were also wet with tears of relief.

The ambulance came soon after. More onlookers had arrived and questions were asked by everyone, including a middle aged policeman. Finally Sheenagh wandered back to the tree at the top of the slope. Ronan was following. The shadows had gone as the evening sunlight blanketed the area.

As they stood under the leaves, she turned to Ronan. "Does that answer your question?"

He seemed puzzled. "Sorry? ... What question?"

"You wondered if being a footballer is all that you are. Remember?"

Ronan paused, touching a hand to his chin, pensively. He

smiled as he considered the answer. "I guess it does."

Sheenagh gave him a moment before continuing. "Shall we get going to the hospital to see how he is? You said you'd give me a lift." Ronan nodded and they began walking to where his car was parked. They stayed by the water's edge, their feet bare on the damp sands. However, within a few yards they were met by a group of teenagers.

"Autographs," Ronan sighed. "At least someone wants my signature. It'll only take a minute or two," he said apologetically to Sheenagh.

Although he readied himself for the group of teenage girls, they ignored him to converge on Sheenagh. Quite a few were clambering for her attention. She grinned at Ronan whose face was a mixture of shock and surprise. His features did not change when they began chatting about their holidays and adventures. Some of her class? One even had a book of poems she asked Sheenagh to autograph. Ronan noticed that Sheenagh's photo was on the back cover.

After the group had left, Sheenagh giggled. "Sorry. They're not into football. Not everyone is, I'm afraid."

"Guess I deserved that. So, tell me, why the giggles?" Ronan enquired.

"You," she laughed. "Your expression was absolutely priceless."

"Yeah," Ronan smiled as he recalled his shock at being ignored. "Sometimes I need reminding that I'm not the biggest 'Starperson' around."

They stopped to watch the sun setting on the horizon. After a minute, Ronan reached out to touch her fingers which she willingly intertwined in his. The sunlight glistened on the water as they both gazed at the waters.

"The white horses have gone," Ronan commented.

"It's okay, they're not far away, they're resting in their seaweed meadows." She knelt down to put her hand into the waves lapping on the beach. Ronan knelt also, placing his hand on hers.

He closed his eyes.

"Yes, I can see them now. They're sleeping ... dreaming."

Sheenagh rested her head on his shoulder.

The gentle sounds of lapping nearby merged with the quietness of dusk. She was almost afraid to ask him, fearing that this magical moment would be shattered but she had to know.

"And ... and will we be here again tomorrow to see them when they come back? You ... and I, together?"

Ronan paused for a moment before kissing her gently on the cheek.

"Oh, yes. White horses couldn't keep me away."

ORIGINAL WRITING
FROM
IRELAND'S OWN

If you have enjoyed this collection of short stories and memoirs, and would like some more, we have some copies left of our previous publications for 2013, 2012, 2011 and 2010 at just €10 per copy, post and packing included.

2010

2011

2012

2013

Contact:

Garrett Bonner, Original Writing, SPADE Enterprise Centre,
North King Street, Dublin 7.
T - 01-6174834 • E - info@originalwriting.ie • W - www.originalwriting.ie